BY SEA

THE WITCHES OF PORTLAND, BOOK FOUR

T. THORN COYLE

Copyright © 2018
T. Thorn Coyle
PF Publishing

Cover Art and Design © 2018
Lou Harper

Editing:
Dayle Dermatis

ISBN-13: 978-1-946476-08-1

BY SEA

When is the cost of bravery too high?

Raquel owns a successful café. She's in a coven. Life is full. Should be good, right?

No. Parenting a teenage boy who is hiding something serious, Raquel is also a witch who doubts her powers. What good are they, anyway?

But the Goddess she's dedicated to won't let her off the hook.

In walks Charlie. Tall, broad shouldered, and crazy handsome. His gaming store has been threatened with violence. And somehow, it's connected to her son...

This is a standalone book in a linked series.
The series can be read in any order.

1

RAQUEL

She looked ahead on the sun-washed shoreline and saw Zion's dark shape, playing chicken with the waves. He knew better than to turn his back on the ocean. Raquel had taught him that early on. The waves on the Oregon coast could reach up and snatch a person before they even knew what happened. Tourists got dragged out to sea at least once a summer.

You'd never see a local standing on a log, just as you'd never see a local turn her back on the sea.

It was good to see Zion having fun, laughing, and running back and forth, filled with the energy of a thirteen-year-old boy. Lately, the smile that usually graced his face had become as rare as sun during the Oregon winter. But he still wouldn't tell her what was wrong.

"It's nothing, Mom," he kept insisting. Well, it was something, that was for sure. And it felt like more than just adolescent blues.

The sand was cool, and crunched under the balls of her feet as Raquel walked, sneakers in hand. She skirted the massive, uprooted trees that dotted the coastline like the corpses of fallen giants. They looked like the bones of some mythical creatures, who lived in a land far away. A land that time forgot.

Her dreadlocks tied back, she turned her face to the sun, and inhaled the brackish scent of salt water and washed-up seaweed. It soothed her heart and soul. The winter had been hard. She was so ready for Beltane and the warmer months.

Raquel hadn't been to the coast in entirely too long. But for a single parent running her own business, days off were in short supply. It didn't matter how busy her life was, though, she always reached the point where she just had to get close to the ocean. She needed her dose of salt water, sea air, and the screech of seagulls flying over the cliffs.

So today, she'd left her coven sister Cassiel in charge of the café, packed Zion into her beetle-green electric Fiat, and made the two-hour drive to Lincoln City.

Just up ahead was a five-foot-tall pyramid of driftwood. People loved to make sculptures of the sea detritus, and the park service always came along and knocked them back down again. The never ending cycling of nature, art, and government rules.

They'd been coming to this beach since Zion was five, after his dad died and Raquel needed to do things that got her away. Zion still loved the kites that flew in bright array when the wind was right. They'd already walked by the kites. Raquel could hear them flapping in the wind behind her. She inhaled, as deeply as she could, and held the breath in her lungs. Then she slowly exhaled. Goddess, her soul needed this. She watched the waves rolling in as she walked, tumbling and crashing into nothingness, until there was just a slender wash of water, snaking up onto the shore.

"Sorry I've turned my back on you lately, Mama." Raquel

said. "You are my heart, my soul. And I know it's been too long."

Yemọja. She of the oceans and the rivers. Siren of the sea. Protector of children and women. Raquel had been dedicated to Yemọja since long before she became a witch. She just hadn't known the Power's name back then.

Raquel had always been a creature of the sea. She even collected mermaids as a child, loving the strangeness of a being that was half human, half massive fish.

Raised a nominal Christian, it was only once she started studying magic—and she and Brenda had formed Arrow and Crescent Coven together—that she began to understand that the ocean had a Goddess. *Was* a Goddess. Or really, what some African peoples called an òrìṣà, a Power. And that Power had a name.

Raquel had worshiped Yemọja ever since.

Zion looked happy. Maybe she just needed to get him out of the city more often. Away from what troubled him. Of course, not every place in Oregon felt safe for a Black mother and her child. Her own mama had taught her that.

"But you can't let that stop you, girl," she murmured to the wind.

White-and-gray gulls swooped down in front of her, and began picking at the shoreline, looking for small crabs. A group of plovers ran towards the water, and then raced back. It was amazing how they moved in concert like that, almost as if they were one being. Kind of like bees, she supposed. She wondered how much individual plover consciousness there was.

Look at you, musing on the deep mysteries of bird brains, she chided herself.

Zion shrieked, and her head snapped towards him again, just in time to see the small wave that had hit him begin to recede. His pants were drenched. Well, she'd planned for that, hadn't she? Making him put extra pants and socks, and a T-shirt even, into his backpack, currently locked in the trunk of the car. You never knew what was going to happen on the coast.

The sun highlighted his limbs, and the shape of his beautiful head. When Zion was young, a local painter had done a portrait of him as a tarot card—The Sun. In the painting, his arms upraised, huge grin on his face, his whole body was outlined by bright golden rays. Just like today. Her sunny boy, he warmed her heart.

Raquel took in another breath and paused on the sand for a moment, turning to face her beloved ocean full-on. The sun was just at her left side, still high, but beginning to wester. She dug her feet into the sand, and dropped her shoes. She raised her own arms to the sky.

"Yemoja! Mother, ocean, water of my heart, of my spit, of my blood. Renew me, let me grow again. Watch over and protect my son, Zion. Whatever troubles his heart, let him know that his mother loves him...and guide me, please. Show me the best way to comfort him, and help him on his path. Yemoja, please bless our family. Give us the strength we need, and give me a sign that I'm on the right track. Blessed be. Ashé."

The light breeze ruffled the edges of her dreadlocks. Raquel needed renewal. Badly. She needed to not always work so hard. And lately? Maybe this was what people called a crisis of faith. She felt at odds with herself. With the coven. And with her own power.

She felt the salt of tears, pricking at the back of her eyes. She blinked them back and took in a shuddering breath. Goddess, so much emotion all of a sudden!

"Mama? Please. Ease this aching in my heart."

A lot of things made her heart ache these days. Another boy had been killed by police, and she was raising a Black son. The climate was still changing, the earth suffering. Some days, it felt as if the whole world were on fire. She needed the cooling waters to bathe her soul.

But that wasn't all.

"And Mama? If it's not too much to ask, maybe even send me someone to love, who will love me back."

There. She'd said the words out loud.

It had been so long since someone had held Raquel at night. So long since she had someone other than her coven and her friends to make her laugh.

Too long since someone had looked at her, just as a woman. Not a parent. Not a priestess. Not their boss. Maybe that was why she felt at odds with her power. She was sick of holding it all the time.

She just needed a damn break.

And the coven had been so serious these days. Their magic had taken a turn in the last year. It was a good thing, but damn, a woman could use some ease and celebration, you know?

And with the trouble Zion was in, whatever it was...? Laughter had been in short supply all around.

Raquel sighed, and pressed her fingers into the corners of her eyes. She wanted love and everything that came with it. She just didn't see how it was going to happen. When did she ever have time to meet someone? And she sure didn't have the energy to waste on those dating apps. She'd heard they were mostly for sex these days, anyway. Not that she had anything against sex, but she did okay for that on her own. She *wanted* sex. But she wanted it mixed in with the possibility of love.

"Zion!" she called across the sand.

His head whipped around, and he grinned, a broad smile filled with white teeth. He ran toward her, feet churning the sand as he went, streaks of it sticking to his wet jeans. Raquel couldn't help but smile.

"Where are your shoes?"

He pointed toward one of the big logs behind her.

"Up there. But Mama, look what I found!"

He held out his hands. In one small palm was a sand dollar, perfect and whole, untouched by the beaks of the seagulls and the ravages of being bashed against the shore. And in the other palm was a beautiful, soft-edged piece of turquoise. Sea glass.

"Oh baby, those are beautiful."

"Hold out your hand," he said.

She did, and he dropped the sea glass into her palm.

"That's for you."

"Thank you baby, I love it." She folded her son into her arms, just for a moment, looking at the ocean over his head. He smelled of the sea, and the sweat of a boy.

As always these days, Zion pulled away first. She wondered how quickly the day was coming that he wouldn't let her hug him in public at all. Soon, she bet.

"You hungry?"

"Yes!"

It was so good to see him happy.

"Let's go get some food, then. Get your shoes on."

As Zion raced to get his sneakers, Raquel turned toward the ocean once again. She held up the sea glass toward the ocean. It glowed in the light of the sun. Luminous.

She hoped this token from the ocean was a sign that good things were coming.

2

CHARLIE

Damn, Charlie loved spring. At least he used to.

The crisp, blue skies. The blooming tulips and cherry trees. The influx of children who overran the shop when they were released from school.

Yeah. It was that time of year. Owlbear Games was swamped with preteens and teenagers, all scoping out the newest games, looking for cards to boost their carefully put-together packs, or eyeing pewter miniatures in the display cases.

Lindsey Sterling played her violin ode to Skyrim over the speakers, and Charlie was ensconced at the far end of the long, glass display counter, behind his computer, working on the books, a steaming cup of milky tea at his right hand.

Sam was at the opposite end, working the register. She was a young Korean American woman with long black hair, two eyebrow piercings, and a black hoodie with a Princess Leia silhouette in red and the caption: "A woman's place is in the resistance."

Sam had been a godsend to Owlbear. Not only was she a

hard worker, she was a geek extraordinaire. Sam knew her stuff, and didn't take shit from the sexist dirtbags that occasionally darkened the shop's door. In her spare time, she DMd tabletop adventures, wrote her own games, and even did some coding. He knew she was secretly hoping to make it big someday.

Charlie had asked her once why she didn't go work for a gaming company, but she insisted she was just messing around. Messing around or scared to put herself out there? Made no difference. Charlie knew better than to push. Everyone grew into themselves in their own time.

"You couldn't die in the middle of winter, could you?" He jabbed at the keys. "You had to die in spring, and throw everything into a tailspin." His father. His beloved, stern, problematic father. It wasn't actually that he had messed up Charlie's favorite season, marking it forever as "when Dad died." It was that Charlie...was overwhelmed by it all.

Charlie took a sip of tea, a cardamom-laced Assam. His favorite tea, on his favorite kind of day, in a shop he now, amazingly, owned free and clear.

Charlie felt like shit.

Owlbear had no mortgage now because Charlie's father had co-signed the building loan six years before. And two weeks ago? His sixty-five-year-old heart had decided to just give up.

David Dillon had left Charlie enough money to pay off the building. So yeah, Owlbear was his now. No one could take it, or his apartment above it, away.

But he'd also left Charlie the legacy of an attic of boxes filled with things Charlie didn't want to think of. Things that troubled him.

He tucked an errant strand of gold-blond hair back

behind his ear and sighed. He really shouldn't be thinking about his father's past. He needed to focus on these books.

Whether a business was doing well or poorly, there were always numbers to crunch. His very non-favorite thing to do, but the end of April was coming pretty damn quick, and if he didn't get all of his receipts entered, Charlie knew he'd be very unhappy come quarter's end. Just because last year's taxes had been filed a month before didn't mean he could slack on this year's accounting.

He really shouldn't be doing accounts in the middle of a rush, but Sam insisted she was fine, and besides, from this vantage point, Charlie could easily keep an eye on the browsing kids without looming. Nothing cleared a shop out more quickly than a looming and suspicious owner.

He also checked periodically on the twenty-somethings back at the gaming tables. A group of white dudes with fancy, high-and-tight hair cuts, with a longer swathe swooping over their foreheads, they'd been coming in more and more lately. They were polite and friendly, but there was something a little off about them. They didn't look like the usual run of nerds.

Besides, they played HackMaster. Charlie never trusted anyone who was into that game.

Not that Charlie hadn't learned to question his prejudices every step of the way in this business.

Prejudices. Yeah. Back to Dad.

His father's funeral had taken place the week before. A lot of his buddies from the VA had attended, gregarious men with haunted eyes. Charlie found he didn't like them much. He felt badly about it, but that was just the truth. Not that Charlie had anything against veterans. Plenty of them came into the shop, and to game nights. But these friends of his father's? Charlie had the eerie sense that they were waiting for some signal from him, as though he was suddenly going to join some secret club.

He had a suspicion about that, but wasn't ready to face it head-on. Maybe some things needed to stay in boxes.

"Look! They have new Magic packs!" One of the kids near the wire spinning racks held up a booster deck, a grin so big on her face you'd think it was Christmas.

Charlie smiled. He loved the preteens most of all. They weren't afraid to be excited about things. They hadn't had their joy slammed out of them against school lockers enough times to beat it out of them. Yet.

The kids were good for his heart and soul.

Sam had told Charlie to take the rest of the month off, but he couldn't stand rattling around his childhood home. It just felt like work. A burden instead of a gift. Heavy with years, emotions, and those damn secrets. The few boxes he'd looked at were almost enough to convince him to shove the bulk of it into a storage space, and get the old Northeast Portland house cleared and cleaned, and...

Charlie wasn't sure what the step after that was. Sell the place? Move in? At any rate, he could ignore the house and the dresser drawers, and the piles of papers, and the boxes of memorabilia for now. No rush, except the fact that it had to get done someday.

He shook his head, then realized he'd entered the same receipt three times already.

"Damn it."

He wasn't good for anything these days. Charlie shoved back from the computer. May as well...do what? His eyes lit on the kids ogling the pewter miniatures.

"You finding what you need?" he asked. "Want to see any of the figures?"

The boy and girl were small, the boy looked Latinx and

the girl was definitely white, with a dirty blond braid down her back. They smelled like bubble gum.

The boy pointed to one of the unpainted figures. An ogre with a battle-ax.

Charlie jingled his keys from his jeans pocket and unlocked the case, carefully picking up the tiny figure between his big fingers.

The kids looked at him with large eyes, brown and hazel. He knew he could be intimidating, with his broad, weightlifter's shoulders and chest covered by a Deadpool T-shirt, blond hair just brushing his shoulders.

"Thanks," the boy said, when Charlie placed the figure in his hand.

"What are your names?"

"Joe," the boy said.

"Tracy," said the girl.

"Do you paint?" Charlie asked.

They both nodded.

"That's great. We just got some new brushes in if you need them."

He led them over to the display that held tiny pots and squeeze bottles of brightly colored paints, and a variety of brushes.

The sound of a *Star Trek* phaser announced that someone had come in the door.

"Sobrino! Are you bothering this man?"

A harried-looking, trim man bustled toward them, a crease on his brow. His dark brown hair was receding and he wore a purple button down shirt over slacks and stylish leather shoes. A younger child followed him, another boy of around seven, if Charlie had to guess.

The new child's eyes grew huge, and he gasped.

"Are you Thor?" he asked.

Charlie laughed.

"Henry!" the man said. He looked embarrassed. "Just because a man has blond hair doesn't mean he's from the movies."

"It's not a problem," Charlie said. "Happens all the time."

He crouched down in front of the boy. "I'm not Thor, but I'm pleased to meet you, Henry. My name's Charlie and I was just showing your...brother?" he looked at the other boy, who nodded. "I was just showing your brother some miniatures and paints."

He stood then, and addressed the man. "Charlie Dillon." He held out his hand. The men shook.

"Alejandro López. Thanks for letting the kids poke around your shop on their own. These are my nephews. The boys go to two different schools now, and one of the other parents told me this was a safe place to meet up."

"We try to make it welcoming for everyone, and the older kids are certainly welcome here on their own. Any younger than eleven or twelve, and we'd worry. But a lot of parents drop their kids here. Feel free to leave your phone number at the desk. We keep a database in case anything goes wrong."

Alejandro's shoulders dropped a little, in relief, Charlie supposed. It had to be hard to be a parent or guardian these days.

The man frowned then, and jerked his head toward the gaming tables near the back.

"Those guys in here a lot?" he asked, dropping his voice.

"Lately," Charlie said.

"They give you any trouble?"

"Not yet. And if they do, I'll make sure they don't come back."

Alejandro shook his head. "Sorry. Maybe it's prejudice, but I just have trouble trusting men who look that way."

Charlie didn't blame him, not with the recent racist knife attacks on the MAX train, and some houseless people getting beaten up at night. Reports were always young white men, clean-cut.

Never caught.

The two men shared a look, before Alejandro nodded, seemingly satisfied for now.

"Joe, you want to ask your uncle if you can get that ogre?"

He left them discussing the miniatures and paints, Joe's voice rising with excitement over the colors he just *had* to have.

Charlie glanced toward the back. One of the men's eyes flicked from Alejandro to Charlie.

Then he smiled. As if he and Charlie were part of some secret club. Just like his father's friends.

And Charlie didn't like that smile at all.

3
___

RAQUEL

It was Cassiel's day off, and Laurel was filling in, making cappuccino and lattes as Raquel started cleaning up the kitchen area. She was a rail-thin woman who loved neo-hippie clothing. Today's outfit consisted of brown leggings, soft brown boots, and a tight T-shirt tunic, patterned with a mandala. Her heavy hair pulled back in a moss-green scarf.

It was a couple hours before closing time. The lunch rush was over, and only a few people were left in the shop, mostly those who used the place as their office.

Ibeyi sang, voices blending over Latin rhythms. Raquel's hips twitched a little, unable to resist moving in time to the groove.

Zion did homework at one of the booths against the wall, backpack on the floor next to him. One hand gripped his natural, and the other was fisted around a pen. He concentrated hard, her boy. She loved that about him. He was so sunny, but so intense as well.

She still wished she knew what was bugging him so badly. The whole ride home from the ocean, she'd been waiting for him to spill, but he only wanted to talk about some new game that had come into the shop down the street from the café, and how excited his friends were about it.

Raquel put lids on the chopped onions and pickles, getting them ready to go back in the huge refrigerator in the break room. The cheeses were already wrapped up and ready to go.

She was grateful to Kelsey, the former owner of the café, for organizing the small kitchen space so well.

Raquel washed her hands for the twenty-fifth time, and felt a rush of a breeze and heard voices. Turning as she dried her hands, she saw what looked like a father and son, a white man and a boy who looked an awful lot like him. They both had ruddy cheeks and pale brown hair. She turned back to her work. Laurel would help them.

"Hey!" She heard Zion's voice and her head snapped around again.

The white boy stood near Zion, and the contents of Zion's pack had spilled out on the floor. She never could get the boy to zip that pack up.

Instead of bending to pick up the spilled pencils and Zion's phone, the white boy stood, feet apart, hands clenched in fists.

What in Goddess's name?

She came out from behind the counter.

"Excuse me?"

The white boy didn't turn, but his father did.

"May I help you?" he asked her.

She looked up. His face was benign. Oh so reasonable looking. But Raquel also noticed he was blocking her way.

"I'm wondering if your son is going to apologize for kicking my son's backpack."

The man ignored her.

"Jeremy!" the man said.

The boy's head whipped around.

"Apologize to that boy. I'm sure you didn't mean to kick his bag. Right?"

The boy and his father exchanged a look. The boy gave a sharp shrug and turned to Zion, who was crouched on the ground, pencils in hand, looking up at Raquel with fear in his eyes.

Blood roared in Raquel's ears and she shoved her way around the white man to stand by her son. Crossing her arms over her chest, she waited, taking in long, careful breaths to slow the angry shaking that was her body's response to not being able to punch something.

"Sorry," the boy mumbled.

"What was that?" Raquel asked. She took another breath, making certain to expand her stomach muscles and engage her diaphragm. Spiritual centering practice 101, just like she taught her students.

The boy shot her a look that was designed to intimidate. She wondered where he had learned that from. Her eyes darted to his father. Yep. Same angry, authoritative look.

Masters of the Universe hated it when the help talked back. Well. They could just deal.

Raquel gave the shields embedded in her aura a quick boost, and stood taller in her boots. A little glamour never hurt.

A flash of uncertainty crossed the boy's face, just as his father nudged his shoulder.

"I'm sorry," the boy said.

"Zion?" she asked.

"Okay," her son said, then went back to picking up his scattered school supplies.

Raquel pasted a large, fake smile on her face. "Why don't

you help Zion to pick up his things, while I take your father's order?"

Yep. Two could play the authority game.

"That's okay, Mom," Zion mumbled.

"Oh no, I'm sure Jeremy will be happy to help. Won't you, Jeremy?" she said, not taking her eyes off of his father.

Enough people were tuned into the situation—including Thomas, who kept watch from behind the counter—that the man would either have to double down or relent. Raquel held his gaze, still smiling. His mouth twisted in a grimace, but his shoulders relaxed enough to signal to her that he was going to relent. Good.

"Help the boy, Jeremy," he said.

Raquel nodded, then moved past him again, and walked toward the counter.

Laurel's eyes were huge, but she still looked ready to act if Raquel needed backup. That was good. They rarely had trouble in the café, but it was nice to know her employees were on top of it, and willing to step forward should the situation require it.

"Thanks, Laurel, I'll take care of this."

Laurel nodded, grabbed a rag, and went to wipe down one of the booths that had emptied out before this all began.

"What can I get you?"

"Black coffee and an apple juice. To go." He spat the words out as though under sufferance. As though he wanted to wrap his well-manicured fingers around her Black neck.

"Coming right up!" she said brightly, then turned to pump a steaming stream of oil-colored coffee into a paper go cup. Asshole.

Jeremy came up behind him as she set the cup on the counter. She looked past the father and son to make sure

Zion was all right. He was. He had moved his backpack to the booth bench, and tapped a pencil on the tabletop. His face looked pinched.

His books were still opened on the table, but he was staring at the man and his son.

Yeah. Expecting him to get back to homework with these predators still in the café was asking too much. Raquel turned to get a juice from the small fridge under the food prep counter.

"I thought we were getting food," Jeremy whined. "I'm hungry."

"Later, Jeremy!" his father said.

The implications were clear. They weren't staying in Raquel's café one moment longer than necessary. Fine with Raquel. She didn't want their money anyway.

She thunked the glass apple juice bottle down next to the coffee and slid a plastic lid next to it.

The man reached toward his pocket, going for his wallet.

"On the house," she said, waving her hand at him. She just wanted them out of there. And most of all, she did not want to touch this man's hands when she passed his change back to him.

He gave a curt nod, shoved the juice at his son's hands, popped the lid onto his coffee cup, and spun on his heel.

He nudged the boy forward, a little too hard, toward the café door.

There was some scuffling as they opened it and moved through, but Raquel had no time to attend to that. She rushed toward Zion's booth and slid in the other side, leaning toward him, voice low.

"You mind telling me what in Goddess's name that was all about?"

Face down, Zion cheated his eyes up toward her, then looked at the tabletop again.

"Zion? Look at me, please." She made her voice as gentle as possible. "That wasn't an accident, was it?"

Zion shook his head, face drawn. Not her sunny boy. Gods. Fury and the wish to hold her precious son close warred inside her.

"Has this been happening at school? Is that what's been wrong with you lately? The thing you keep not telling me about?"

"Can't we just drop it, Mom?"

She grabbed onto his arm with her left hand, and with her right, tilted his chin up, forcing him to look into her eyes.

She heard the door open, but didn't look up to see who was entering. She dropped her hand from his chin and sighed.

"No. We can't just drop it. It's my job to protect you, Zion. And I can't help do that if you won't tell me what's going on."

"There isn't anything you can do, okay?"

"Zion, there is *always* something we can do! But we have to face the situation first. Isn't that what I've always told you?"

That wasn't one-hundred-percent true, but he would learn that soon enough. For now, she needed him to believe. To believe in his power. To believe in himself.

Just like she was supposed to.

Zion looked down at the table again, and nodded. Goddess, he looked so miserable. Her heart broke in half.

Who the hell was doing this to her baby boy? And why?

4
____

CHARLIE

It was another truly gorgeous Portland day: blue sky, sunshine, people out on the sidewalk, laughing, taking advantage of the break in the rain.

"You cool with Raquel's for lunch?" Hai asked. Hai was a friend and colleague both. A cool-looking guy with tattoos down his arms and a spiky brush of shining black hair, he ran a games and comic book store in northeast Portland.

"Sounds good to me," Charlie responded. Raquel's made the best sandwiches in the neighborhood, but he tried not to go there too often because if he had to admit it to himself, he'd developed a little thing for Raquel. He'd never said anything, because he figured *everyone* had a little thing for Raquel. Besides, she was so busy all the time. He knew she had a kid, Zion. He'd started coming around Owlbear lately. Charlie never saw a dad around, though, not that that meant anything.

As they approached the café, he could see people inside through the windows. He was about to reach for the door when it burst open and a white man shepherded his son out with a little shove.

"Why'd you do that?" the man said.

"He's a big dork. Everyone hates him," the kid replied. His face was petulant, the corners of his mouth turned down.

Charlie watched as the man's fingers gripped the kid's shoulder, a little too hard. The kid winced, then set his face into a mask.

"Never in public." The man practically spat out the words.

Charlie looked down at the kid. The kid looked up, then down again, his pale cheeks flushing with shame at being caught out. The dad cut his eyes at Charlie, dismissed him as no threat, and looked back down the boy.

"How many times do I have to tell you..."

"Hey kid?" Charlie asked. The man's and the boy's heads both snapped towards him, startled to be interrupted. "You like games? I run the shop down the street. We have gaming every afternoon and you're always welcome to come."

Charlie held out a small, postcard-sized flyer with Owlbear's information on it. The kid started to reach for it, but the father's hand intercepted it, snapping it out of Charlie's hand.

"Thanks man," he said with a stern nod. "Let's go, Jeremy." He gave the boy another little shove and they walked off down the sidewalk. The kid's shoulders were hunched up around his ears. The father walked, stiff as a board, beside him.

Charlie shook his head, then turned to Hai. "I hate dudes like that."

Hai nodded, lips tight. "I do too, man. But some parents are assholes, we all know that. Or maybe they're just strict, I don't know."

Charlie sighed and opened the door, waiting for Hai to

walk through. He knew strict; that hadn't looked like strict. As they walked in, he saw Raquel sitting at a booth with Zion, intent on their conversation. Looked serious. So they walked to the counter and place their order with Laurel, who looked mildly rattled, though she offered them a huge smile. Once they were settled, Charlie broached the subject.

"So, there's kind of no beating around the bush with this..."

"But you're going to anyway, ha?" Hai gave him a little smile and took a big drink of his cappuccino, foam dotting his dark upper lip. Charlie motioned to his face, and Hai picked up a napkin and swiped.

Charlie took a sip of his own coffee. Black, just the way he liked it. Though his stomach was starting to complain about that. He figured he'd have to start adding milk or something pretty soon.

He set down the red ceramic cup again. "Is your shop having trouble with Nazis?"

"You mean like the Gamer Gate dudes?"

"Yeah... Them, but tabletop players, too. Or any of the fascist dudes. You know, the ones that love the fake Spartan history graphic novels."

Hai sat back in his chair, and looked off towards the windows. Charlie tried to tune out the sounds in the café. Some women with French accents sang over a rolling Latin beat, the sound coming from the small speakers set in the corners of the room. There was the quiet hum of conversations, the hiss of the milk steamer, and the clatter of computer keys. He tried to focus on Hai's face. So he wouldn't get distracted.

Hai finally looked back. Then he tapped his lips with one narrow finger. Charlie's gaze was caught by the slim gold band of Hai's wedding ring. Finally, his friend spoke.

"There's nothing exactly, not that I can prove.... But there is a group I've been watching. They been coming in about once a week for the last, oh, I don't know, six months?"

"White guys? Intense haircuts?"

Hai nodded. "But who *isn't* dealing with them right now? It's like every white asshole has crawled out from beneath a rock lately."

"Well, shit. I was hoping it was just my shop. And beyond that, I was actually hoping I was just being paranoid and stupid. And there's something else."

Charlie slide a white index card across the table. He had carefully written down some symbols on it. Symbols he didn't understand.

"Someone has been scrawling these on our bathroom walls, and on the poles outside the shop. Do they look familiar?"

Hai frowned, then shook his head. "Not really. I mean, they're runes, I know that much. But I can't tell you what they mean or anything. Norse."

"So, more white nationalist stuff."

"Damn those guys, anyway."

Laurel set their grilled panini sandwiches down on the table. Both men nodded their thanks and settled in to eat. Charlie knew that this was Hai's way of processing. He always needed to let the wheels turn in silence, kind of the opposite of Charlie. Charlie had learned to wait.

He and Hai been friends for a long time. Even though folks thought they should be rivals, they've never been anything but friends. Hai was just decent people, and a smart businessman to boot. Charlie had learned a lot from him about how to run Owlbear. They'd started working on plans for a citywide Geek Week for the coming fall. Half a sandwich in, Hai wiped his mouth, cleared his throat, and looked up.

"I think with everything else going on, we need to take this seriously. We need to ask all the gaming and comics shops if they're having trouble, and we need to figure out what to do."

Charlie slumped with relief. "I hate that you're confirming this is true. But on the other hand? I'm glad you're up for this. Thanks, man."

Hai held out a hand and turned it upside down and back again, showing off one slim, tattooed arm that was nevertheless several shades darker than Charlie's own.

"My grandparents are from China, man. You think those dudes you're talking about *like* me? The only reason they come to my shop is that I'm the only place in the neighborhood. But I have no illusions, man. Once they get through the Blacks, the Jews, and the immigrants from Guatemala and Mexico, I'm pretty sure my family is up next."

Then Hai picked up the other half of his sandwich and crunched through the grilled bread into the ham and spinach and cheese.

Damn. Charlie shoved his plate away. His stomach felt too tight to eat all of a sudden.

"So what are we gonna do?"

"We'll figure it out, man. And then we'll kick some Nazi ass."

5

RAQUEL

Raquel slammed through the kitchen like an avenging Fury. She had planned to cook chicken for dinner, but was too angry to do more than fill a pot with water and bang it onto the stove, then turn on the gas and crash a lid down on top.

Pasta sauce from a jar would have to do. She did add onion, garlic, rosemary, and some spices to the pan, and chopped up a couple of chicken sausages to add to the mix, but she sure as hell wasn't doing elaborate cooking tonight. Not that she ever had much energy for it on work evenings, but still. She tried to avoid relying on the single parent stock-in-trade too often.

At least it wasn't hot dogs on white bread buns.

"Mom..." Zion stood in the kitchen doorway.

Raquel stopped, put her hands on the white countertop, and forced herself to take a deep breath and look at her son.

He'd shucked his jacket and backpack, and stood in an Invader Zim T-shirt and blue jeans, feet bare on the Spanish tile floors. His afro was a mess as usual. She never could convince him to pick it out evenly. She supposed that was the current kid style.

Goddess, listen to her. You'd think she was seventy instead of thirty-five. Raising a child and running a business aged a person, though. There was no denying it.

"Yes, Zion?" She pitched her voice low and even. She didn't want to direct the anger his way, though she was a little pissed that it had taken him so long to tell her what was happening.

"You okay?"

Well, shit. Of course her son the empath would feel the emotional maelstrom whirling through the house. Not that it took an empath to hear the crashes. Zion had picked up on other people's emotional states since he was a baby. They'd worked on shielding and centering for years, but it was hard to maintain your boundaries when it was your own damn mother making a ruckus.

"I'm...no. I'm not okay. I'm angry. Really, really, angry."

And exhausted with it. Another problem, piled on top of all her other responsibilities. Plus, they were messing with her son.

Yemoja, you listening? You gonna help me out?

He inched his way into the kitchen and pulled out one of the oak chairs that ringed the four top table in the center of the room. The table and chairs had graced her own grandmother's kitchen, long ago. Raquel and Zion had sanded and stained them together, just a couple of years before.

He stared down at the table, tracing the grain with one dark finger. "You mad at me?"

Raquel sighed, and turned the heat down under the sauce, giving it a stir. The pasta water needed some time before it came to a boil, so she pulled out a chair for herself, then reached across and squeezed Zion's hand.

"I'm not angry with you, Zion. I feel worried. Worried and upset. And I'm angry that someone is hurting you."

He was still staring at the table.

"Hey. Can you look at me?"

He did. She could see the pain in his dark brown eyes. His face was still round and slightly chubby, but Raquel could see the planes of cheekbones beginning to emerge, and his forehead was becoming more defined. But Goddess, he was still so young.

"I am a little upset that you didn't tell me sooner. That I had to find out because that boy kicked your backpack over today. Did you feel like I wouldn't understand?"

Zion shrugged his shoulders. The lid on the pasta pot began to clatter, signaling that the water was on the boil. Raquel stood and poured a dollop of olive oil into the salted water before dumping in the pasta. She stirred the dry noodles carefully, ensuring that they separated and that every strand was fully submerged. Then she turned the heat down a tick, set the timer on her watch, and turned back to her son.

"Well?"

"I just...didn't want to bug you. You always have so much going on. Especially lately."

And Raquel knew exactly what he was talking about. The past months had been intense with the coven. They'd had a lot to contend with, including government corruption, sweeps of houseless people, and most recently, a woman broadcasting her psychic trauma onto a bunch of unprepared empaths in the city. Raquel was just grateful that Zion hadn't been affected by her. Some of their training was holding, at least.

No matter how much she tried to shield him from it, of course he knew she felt overwhelmed.

And as an empath, Zion was loathe to share his feelings. He didn't want to be a burden on anyone.

It was time to fix that.

"I'm your mother, Zion. You don't have to protect me. As a matter of fact, I'm the one who's supposed to be protecting *you*. You can *always* come to me for help, no matter what. The day I'm too busy for you is the day I'm dead."

She grinned at him then. "And even then, I'll probably hover around for a while, making sure you're okay."

He gave her a small grin in response, but she could tell his heart wasn't in it. Her wrist buzzed. Pasta was done.

"Get the plates, will you?"

Once the pasta was served, and the parmesan was on the table, they bowed their heads over their plates.

"Thank you to the earth, the sun, and the rain. Thank you to every hand that cared enough to bring this food to our table. May all who are hungry, be fed." Zion and Raquel both recited the prayer together, voices mingling in the air. "Blessed be. Ashé."

The sauce smelled good, fragrant with the rosemary and tomato and the hint of chili powder mixing with the onion, garlic, and herbs. It tasted pretty good, too.

Zion had heaped a mound of parmesan onto his pile of sauce and noodles and was twirling a fork in the mess. Thank the Gods he still ate dinner like a normal thirteen-year-old boy.

"So, what do you want to do about these bullies?" Raquel asked. "Do you want me to come into school and talk to your teachers? Or I could contact the students' parents. Are they all boys, doing this to you?"

Zion froze for a moment, then shoved a huge bite into his mouth. Buying time by chewing. That was okay. Raquel didn't blame her son. But she wasn't going to let him off the hook, either.

Finally, he swallowed, and stuck his fork into the pasta, twirling another bite around the tines.

"Zion. Before you take another bite of that spaghetti, I want you to answer me."

His fork clattered to the plate.

"Yes, they're all boys. But I don't want you doing anything yet. Can't you just...?"

"Can't I just what?"

"Make me a charm or something? Do something to my energy field to make me less of a dork?"

Raquel considered her son for a moment. His eyes still looked wounded, but held a flash of anger now, too. Good. Angry was better than cowed.

"First off, you aren't a dork."

He snorted at that, and picked up his fork again.

"Second, though, that's not a bad idea. We can set some sigils into your aura to protect you. I'll need to work on that. We can figure out the right ones together. It might take until sometime this weekend, though."

He nodded, mouth full of spaghetti. Sauce pooled in the corners of his mouth.

"Wipe your mouth when you're done chewing," she said absently. "But we need something in the meantime, don't we?"

She twirled some noodles and sauce onto her own fork, then put the tidy bundle in her mouth and chewed. Raquel felt the chair beneath her. Felt the table, supporting the plates.

Felt her grandmother's presence. Of course.

"Actually, I think sigils aren't the answer. Grandma Rose is here. Do you feel her?"

He nodded.

"We need to call on the ancestors for help. We're going to pray you up every morning before school. Okay?"

Zion was staring at her, as if he were evaluating her words. Goddess, her boy was so smart. So perceptive. It was a miracle he could cope with this world at all, though. The world was hard on smart, sensitive boys. Especially when those boys were Black. But they were just going to have to make sure he was better prepared, weren't they?

"Yeah," Zion finally said. "That sounds good."

6

CHARLIE

Sam was in the back room, going through stock. Charlie wondered if he should call her out front again. Owlbear was filling up with the after-school rush.

No group of twenty-something white guys today, at least, so that was good. After his conversation with Hai, Charlie felt even less easy about them hanging around. But until he and Hai figured out a game plan, he wasn't going to confront the guys. For now, it was enough that they weren't here.

Twin Shadow crooned softly over the speakers as Charlie made room for more miniatures in the locked display case. He placed a tiny, pewter mage in flowing long robes on the shelf, and then figured he should attend to the customers, making sure the kids weren't checking out games their parents wouldn't appreciate them having access to.

He locked the glass case again and went to make sure the board games were still in order. Stuff always got moved throughout the day, and it was constant work to keep things where they could be easily found. And to make sure nothing had made its way out of the store without getting paid for.

A group of tweens pored over tabletop DM books. Two

white boys, a Latinx girl, and an Asian boy. Charlie loved the mix of kids who came in. He and Sam tried to make Owlbear as welcoming to as many nerdy kids as possible, from every race and class.

Portland was never going to be a racially mixed utopia, but damn it, the geeks could do their part. One of the things he and Hai had talked about was making sure there were Black, Asian, Latinx, and queer DMs whenever possible, both in the shops on a weekly basis, but especially for city-wide events like Geek Week.

A good dungeon master made all the difference to a game, and their background influenced the play. Even though people would say "a geek is a geek"—and sure, on one hand, that was true—a trans Latina was still going to make different choices than a cis white dude.

"You need any help there?" he asked the group.

"No. Thanks. We're good. But...do you know of any new DM books coming out?"

Charlie paused a moment. "Yeah, there are two new games coming out next month. Are you on the list?"

"Nah." The girl shook her dark head, hands clutching at her backpack straps. "I'll just check back."

"Okay," Charlie said. "You're Linda, right? And Trevor, Zachary, and Kim?"

The kids nodded, looking pleased that he'd remembered. They'd only started coming in a month ago, and weren't yet regulars at game nights.

"We're running a game you might be interested in this Saturday. It's a cool game about colonization."

"Oh yeah, my brother told me about that," Linda said. "What time?"

"One o'clock."

The phaser over the door sounded, and Charlie turned. It was Zion, Raquel's son.

And he had a busted lip, a scrape along one cheek, and looked as if he was about to burst into tears.

Charlie moved rapidly toward him.

"Zion! You okay?"

The boy just shook his head. He was barely holding it together.

"Give me a second, okay?"

Zion nodded, and just stood there in the middle of the aisle between the multisided dice and the board games.

The kids stared at him for a moment before going back to the gaming manuals, giving him some privacy.

Charlie called Sam's number. "Can you come out front and cover things?"

He got her affirmative and turned back to Zion, who had started to shake.

"Sam's coming to cover the floor, and as soon as she's up here..."

Sam burst out of the back, hoodie unzipped over a red *Star Trek* T-shirt, banged-up Doc Martens eating up ground through the gaming area. As she approached the the front of the shop she burst out, "Holy shit, Zion! You okay?"

She reached out her arms as though she was going to sweep him into a hug.

That was all the boy could handle. Tears ran down his cheeks as he shook his head.

Charlie gave Sam a look and she stopped mid-reach, and cleared her throat.

"I'm just going to take Zion here back to the restroom and clean up these cuts," Charlie said. "Can you handle the front?"

The kids by the books were staring openly now and

Charlie had to get Zion away.

"Of course," Sam said.

Charlie put a gentle hand on Zion's shoulder. "Why don't you leave your backpack with Sam? She can put it behind the counter where it's safe. Okay?"

Zion nodded, sniffing back a trail of liquid that had just started to emerge from his nose. He swung the heavy pack off and Charlie caught it. What the hell did kids keep in those daypacks of theirs? Damn. Charlie handed it off to Sam and, hand on Zion's shoulder, steered him through the game tables to the restroom in the back. The single stall ADA compliant room was big enough for both of them.

He grabbed the first aid kit from the tall cabinet in the corner that held extra toilet paper and cleaning supplies.

"Why don't you wash your hands, then get some water on a paper towel, will you?" Charlie asked.

Zion startled, then complied, turning on the taps and running his hands under the water. He stood, mesmerized, as the water gushed across his fingers and down the drain.

"Hey, buddy? The soap pump is to your right."

Zion moved as though in a daze. Must be in shock. But at least the boy's hands were clean now.

Charlie washed and dried his own hands, then wet a brown paper towel and gently dabbed at Zion's cheek. The lip was going to need ice. They'd get to that later.

"So, you gonna tell me what happened?"

"Got jumped."

"Someone you know?"

He rinsed the paper towel in cold water and handed it to Zion. "Hold that to your lip. It'll have to do, until we can get some ice on your face."

"Same kids as always."

Charlie paused in unscrewing the lid from a tube of antiseptic ointment.

"Same kids? You mean, this has happened before?"

"Not this bad, but yeah."

Damn it. It was always the sweet ones who got the shit kicked out of them. Charlie should know. It was why he'd started lifting weights in the first place. He wanted to become big enough that no one would fuck with him again.

He bent his knees so he could stare into Zion's eyes on the same level. The white LED lamp above the sink mirror was harsh, showing the red tinge around Zion's eyes and nose, the scrape on his cheek. The pain and fear.

"Listen, I don't know exactly what we're gonna do yet, but we'll figure something out, okay?"

Zion sniffed and nodded again, holding the wet paper towel gingerly against his lip. The left side of his face was already starting to puff out. Charlie noticed that the kid's *Star Wars* T-shirt was ripped near the collar.

"How many kids?"

"Three."

"Cowards."

Charlie felt a cold rage settle into his chest and belly. Goddamn bullies. It didn't matter how old they were, they thought they ran the world.

"You ready to go see your mom?"

"Do I have to?"

Charlie stood up again. "Yeah, Zion. She's gonna find out eventually anyway, as soon as she sees your face. So we may as well tell her now."

He dabbed some ointment on the boy's cheek, threw the paper towels away, and secured the first aid kit back in the tall cabinet.

"But if you want to sit behind the counter and ice your face for a while first, that's okay by me."

7

RAQUEL

The door to the café opened, and Zion walked in, face turned to the black-and-white-tiled floor.

The sounds of the café ceased, replaced by a loud ringing. Her vision tunneled, dark around the edges, as though she might faint.

"Oh my Goddess! What happened?" A clammy sweat broke out all over Raquel's body. Her son. What did they do to her son?

Zion's precious face was bloody. He held an ice pack against his cheek and his lip was swollen. He was followed by Charlie, the tall, built, blond man who ran the gaming shop down the street.

Charlie hovered over her son, guiding him into the cafe. Raquel's heart twinged at the sight of it. Something a bit lower twinged, as well, but she pushed the sensation aside and ran to her son.

"Was it that boy?" she asked, moving his hand and the ice pack so she could examine his face. It looked so terrible, she wanted to weep.

There was a bandaged cut over his eye, and a wide

scrape marred his perfect cheek, tracing the incipient line where his cheekbone would be once his face took on its adult shape. She hoped there wouldn't be any scarring. The darkness of a bruise already surrounded the raw, abraded skin, a bluish purple against the brown.

Raquel cringed just looking at it, then released Zion's hand. He put the ice back on his cheek, wincing at the pressure. Zion still hadn't answered her question. Her mouth formed a tight line on her face and she looked up at the handsome white man standing in front of her, arms on her son's shoulders.

Why were his hands on Zion's shoulders? Proprietary. Protective. The way a father would be.

"Did this happen at your store?" she spat out.

"No. He arrived this way. I just cleaned him up and gave him the ice pack."

She turned back to Zion, barely aware of the café sounds resuming around her, smelling only the bacterial ointment Charlie must have slathered on the cut, not the coffee or the scent of grilled sandwiches.

"Was. It. That. Boy?"

He nodded, avoiding her eyes.

"That's it. We're going to Brenda's to get you an amulet. And tomorrow, I'm going to talk to your school."

"Mom!" Zion's head jerked up, a look of panic in his eyes. "Please. Don't."

"Don't what?"

"Don't call my school. Things are bad enough as it is."

"We can't just let the bullying continue, Zion!" She felt angry and exasperated all at once. She was also suddenly aware that she was standing in the middle of her place of business, in front of a man she barely knew other than as a customer.

A man she had no business all of a sudden feeling this attracted to. When in Goddess's name had *that* happened?

"We'll discuss this later. But we *are* going to Brenda's... Oh, damn."

"What's wrong?" Charlie asked.

"My car is in the shop until tomorrow. Well, looks like we're taking the bus, Zion."

Charlie held up a hand.

"My car is just around the block. I don't need to be back at the shop until seven, to run a game tonight."

Raquel held a hand to her forehead, all of the adrenaline that had flushed her body suddenly gone.

"Okay. Thanks. Give me a minute." She walked back to the counter, where her coven sister stood, concerned look on her face.

"Cassiel, are you okay to close on your own? Or can you call in Laurel or something?"

"Of course I can close," Cassiel replied. "It hasn't been that busy today. You go ahead."

"Thanks."

Raquel grabbed her light jacket and purse from the office and returned. Zion was still standing there, with Charlie's hand on his shoulder.

Well. She'd make time to think about that later. Meanwhile, thank the Gods for trustworthy workers who were also part of your coven.

8

CHARLIE

The ride to Hawthorne and Brenda's shop was quick. Charlie could tell Raquel was biting her tongue. Other than telling him where the Inner Eye was located, she'd been lost in her own thoughts.

He found a spot to park on a residential street just around the corner from the busy shopping street.

A flier taped to a light pole caught his eye. "White Pride is Pride in Self."

"Fuckers." He slid his fingers beneath the tape and ripped. Raquel came up behind him.

"What's that?"

"Just a little white nationalist bullshit."

She shook her head, dreadlocks moving heavily over her shoulders. "That shit is everywhere these days. Does it feel like it's getting worse?"

"It does."

She put an arm around her son and led the way down the sidewalk, before calling over her shoulder, "Put that in the garbage, where it belongs."

Charlie could not agree more, and balled up the offending paper, tossing it into an open can on the corner.

There was a guy selling beaded jewelry from a rug on the corner, and Charlie's favorite bookstore was just across the street, along with the old, Moroccan-style movie theater where he and the other geeks stood in line for the big superhero and action flicks when they came out.

He followed the sway of Raquel's full hips down the sidewalk. Somehow, seeing her with Zion made her even more attractive than before, which was funny, because, although he liked kids, he'd never thought of having any of his own.

She pushed her way into a store he'd noticed before, but never been in. It was one of those new-agey-type shops with Tarot cards and crystals in the windows.

As soon as he walked in, it hit him. The air felt different. Cleaner. More clear. Even the slight curls of smoke from incense burning behind the counter didn't mar it.

And the place smelled good. Whatever had been coiled inside Charlie's belly the minute Zion walked into Owlbear with his busted-up face, relaxed. Actually, Charlie realized, he'd been tense for days. Maybe there was something to all this woo stuff.

An attractive woman who looked as if she was in her early forties was cooing and fussing over Zion as Raquel talked with a younger white woman with a head that was shaved except for a long fall of purple hair.

He decided to look around the shop, wandering toward the books. His eyes scanned the shelves. There were books on angels. Books on Tarot. Something called Kabbalah, whatever that was. And yep. Right there. Big as life. A fat red book with *Norse Magic* on the spine, sitting next to an amber gold book, face out, with symbols all over the cover. *Runes from the World Tree*, it read.

He picked it up, and started flipping through it. The symbols danced across the pages, half familiar, half foreign.

"Tiwaz," he read. "The spear of justice."

Pulling the index card from his jacket pocket, he saw that was one of the runes he'd written down, along with one that looked like a jagged slash of lightning. He flipped through the book, searching for that shape.

"Sowilo." The sun.

"Oh. Fuck," he murmured. He hadn't recognized it scrawled on the bathroom wall because he was used to seeing the symbol printed in thick, squared-off lines. And he was used to seeing it in sets of two. "The SS."

The Schutzstaffel. Hitler's Stormtroopers. The real shit that *Star Wars* baddies were modeled after.

So what was a fascist book like this doing in the shop of one of Raquel's friends? He looked around and noticed that the woman who'd been talking with Raquel's son, Zion, was now standing a yard from him, arms crossed over her chest. Dark brown hair fell in waves toward her shoulders. Her eyes were a startling blue. He felt himself flush, as though he'd been caught out.

"You interested in the runes?" she asked, then held out her right hand. "My name is Brenda. Raquel's friend. I own this shop."

He shook her hand, then cleared his throat. "I'm actually a little surprised to see this book here. I mean…" He swept a hand around the brightly lit, comfortable store, with its cozy reading chairs, shelves of books and herbs, and some sort of Irish-tinged harp music soothing the customers pawing through crystals and tchotchkes.

She gave him a discerning gaze, as though she were

about to take his measure. He had no doubt she could do just that, and was oh so not surprised that she and Raquel were friends. They both had that confident, calm air about them. They saw through bullshit and weren't afraid to call a person on it. At least, that had always been Charlie's impression of Raquel, and one of the reasons he found her attractive. And one of the reasons he'd never asked her out.

This woman, Brenda, different as she was from Raquel on the surface, had the same qualities.

"What do you mean?" she asked. "It's a good book."

"Isn't this some Nazi stuff?"

"It can be, just like any system can be. But the runes are far older than that. Hitler and his cronies took the ancient magic and twisted it to their own ends. The runes can be used for communication, for healing, and for creation, just as easily as they can be used for destruction."

He nodded. That made sense to him.

"So," she asked, "why the interest?"

He handed her the index card. "People have been drawing symbols around my shop."

Her mouth pinched itself tight, and her eyes narrowed.

"I hate to see people using the symbols this way." She looked up at him. "And I hate to say this, too, but you should start wearing protection. Maybe ask Raquel to help you protect your shop, too."

"Protection?"

She gave him a slight smile, and led him over to where Raquel and Zion stood, peering over something laid out on the long glass counter.

"Magic," she said. "Cleansing. Amulets. Symbols. Spheres of energy around your space. Sounds like you could likely use it all."

"But..."

As they got closer, Raquel looked up. For the first time ever, she looked lost to him. Small. Not the sexy badass he'd always seen before. Charlie felt gripped with an urge to pull her into his arms. To hold her and protect her. To protect Zion, too.

They shared a look over Zion's head, but Charlie wasn't sure exactly what it meant.

"Did you find the right amulet yet?" Brenda asked.

Zion held up what looked like a pewter-bound piece of hematite. Charlie recognized the gray stone because someone had ordered specialty gaming dice made of the dense substance.

"That's good. It will give you strength and help turn whatever negativity is coming at you into something more useful."

"That's what I told him," Raquel said. "It'll head the nastiness off at the pass."

Charlie had a hard time not rolling his eyes. He respected Raquel, but this was all a bit much.

He cleared his throat. "You ever think of enrolling him in martial arts?"

Raquel looked down at her son. "You tried karate, but didn't like it, right?"

Zion nodded.

"Well, maybe we can research something else."

"I know some guys who say they're doing African-based martial arts," Charlie said. "I have no idea what that looks like, but I can tell you they're cool. They come into the shop with their kids sometimes."

"Could you get us an introduction?" Raquel asked.

"Of course." It felt as if circumstances were winding their lives together, as if a giant hand was moving pieces around a chess board, or as if the dungeon master had decided their quests needed to converge. *Don't get ahead of yourself, Charlie. She's just trying to do what's best for her son.*

"Now, let's talk about protection for you, shall we?" Brenda asked.

Charlie looked at his watch. "I'm going to have to wait on that. I've got to get back to the shop and set up for a game soon. But I *will* buy this book, if you recommend it."

Brenda took the book from his hands, and moved to the cash register.

"Raquel, if it's okay with you, I'd like to take you and Zion out for dinner sometime...." He ran his fingers through his hair, suddenly nervous. "Or maybe, if you want to...just you."

Zion stifled a grin. Charlie swore three different expressions passed across Raquel's face at once.

Finally, she smiled. "We'll talk about it, but I think I should be taking *you* out to dinner."

Raquel put a hand on his arm, and looked straight into his eyes. Her own eyes were a rich, dark brown, with just the hints of tiny lines starting around the corners. Laugh lines. He liked them.

"Charlie? Thanks so much for taking care of my son today."

"Any time."

9

RAQUEL

Raquel should have been with the rest of Arrow and Crescent coven tonight, planning their Beltane ritual, but she just wasn't in the mood. There was no way she could focus on sex, and spring, and the renewal of love and life right now. Brenda had quickly stepped in and offered to host, so Raquel was off the hook.

It wasn't good. It wasn't easy to give up her coven responsibilities like that. But poisoning the coven meeting with her rage wasn't going to be helpful. She couldn't ask them to caretake her emotions in that way.

Her crisis of faith seemed to be deepening.

Today? She was pissed off at witchcraft. Pissed off at the Gods and Goddesses who were not doing their damn jobs, protecting Zion. What good was witchcraft, if the son of a "powerful witch" was coming home with a split lip and swollen face?

And what good was she?

"Power, my ass."

She was so angry. Raquel could barely look at the altar set up on the table in her bedroom corner.

Oh, she knew exactly what was on it. The candles. The ancestor photos. The strings of dotted cowrie shells and the two pearlescent abalone shells, one filled with water, one filled with the burning incense she had thought might clear her head. The athamé, the wand, the cup, the dish. All of the trappings of a witch of African descent, dedicated to Yemoja.

"What good is all of this?" she asked the room, as she paced the space from bed, to the window alcove that held the altar, and back to the dresser on the other side of the room. A three-pointed path. Bed. Altar. Dresser. Dresser. Altar. Bed.

She had known Zion was troubled, but hadn't known he was in danger. Not like this. All of her psychic skills, all of her parenting juju, and she hadn't been able to figure it out. Damn her boundaries anyway. Respecting Zion's privacy.

Sparing his feelings had gotten them into this mess. He just hadn't wanted to tell her, even after that damn white boy had kicked his backpack over. And after getting jumped and beaten? He *still* didn't want her to do anything about the situation.

But oh, she would.

She thought of the binding Selene had done on Caroline's ex-husband after he kidnapped her. That was the last coven crisis, and one that had settled itself to good effect. Caroline was now Brenda's girlfriend, and starting to set up her life here in Portland. So, tricky as the magical operation was, sometimes bindings worked.

Was binding the answer here? Raquel just didn't know. Her brain was too scrambled with rage to know what the correct course was. All she wanted to do was raise a tsunami, obliterating Zion's enemies in one huge flood.

Anger was not her usual mode, but damn, threaten her

son? Face her wrath. If only Zion would let her direct her rage where it belonged: at the kids and their parents, and at the teachers who weren't making certain he was safe at school.

Zion would come around eventually. But for now, she had to channel her anger somewhere. Somehow.

May as well use her training. At least try to.

Goddess, she thought. When you were angry at the very things you relied on for help, what were you supposed to do?

Just...do something, Raquel.

So she lit a candle on the altar. Breathed in the spicy scent of burning incense. Then she picked up a rattle made of dried goat's hooves tied to a smooth stick. Raquel shook that rattle, one hard shake. The hooves clacked and clattered against one another. She shook it again, and stomped one foot on the bare wood floor. Then her other foot. She felt her way into the rhythm of her anger and her rage. She felt her way into the beat of her helplessness. She needed to dance this through. Move it out of her body.

Sometimes working through the body was the only way to clear the heart and mind. Raquel just prayed it worked this time.

Allowing her attention to drift deeper toward her center, she did her best to simply ride the emotions, blending them into the rhythm created by her hands and feet.

"Yemọja. I'm pissed off at you. But I need you. Come to me. Mother Ocean. Come." Her throat was still tight with anger. Too soon to speak. Raquel deepened her movements, pounding her heels onto the floor.

With a sharp jerk of the wrist, she snapped the hooves against each other and stomped her feet. Snap. Stomp. Stomp. Snap. Snap. Stomp. Stomp. Snap.

Closing her eyes, she allowed her whole body to give over to the rhythm of it. Shaking out her anger. Her fear. Her helplessness. Her rage. She shook it all out, toward the burning candle. Toward the glowing incense in the abalone shell. Toward the pool of salty water.

She swallowed. Licked her lips. Tested out her words again.

"Mama. Release me. Mama. Strengthen me. Mama. Surround me. Mama. Fill me up. Fill me up. Fill me with your power."

Back and forth she rocked and stomped and moved. Shaking. Rattling. Breathing. She began to sweat.

The power of Yemoja emerged, flooding the room like the ocean flowed across sand. Yemoja. Taking her. Surrounding her. Filling her. Yemoja. Pure power. Pure fury. Pure grace. Waves. Grabbing. Grasping. Tumbling. Crashing.

Blackness. Submersion. The ocean pulled her down. Raquel fell heavily to the floor, the rattle rolling to the side.

A great cry filled her body, pouring from her mouth. "Aaaiiiiiiiiieeee. Hooooooo. Aaaaiiiiiiiiiii!" Sobbing. Heartrending pain. Broken. She felt broken in two.

A sound. The bedroom door opening. The soft, warm scent of her son. Gentle hands, shaking her shoulders.

A voice, coming as if through layers of water.

"Mom! Mom! What's wrong?"

Then gone. Swept away.

No sound now but the ocean's roar. No scent but ocean brine. No taste but salt and wetness. No vision but Her face. Skin so dark it was almost black, and glowing with strange, fluorescent light, like the creatures that lived at the very bottom of the ocean. Thick braids coiled around her head, threaded through blue and green glass beads. Full hips and breasts and belly, swathed in seaweed and algae that flowed around her like a skirt. A branch of coral wound around the dark column of her neck.

A hand reached out to touch Raquel's face. Her voice boomed through the water, penetrating Raquel's soul.

:Your anger can trap or cleanse you. Your rage can bind you, or set you free. Choose what you desire. Harness the depths of your ocean. The depth of love. Love is the root of your power.:

"Love is the root of my power."

:I am the wave of your heart.:

"Wave."

The Goddess reached out her other hand, grasping Raquel's face, pressing on her cheeks and temples, black eyes boring into her. *:Live in power, my sister. Know your worth. Look to those with strong intentions. Help will come.:*

The vision faded. The ocean faded. The scent of candle wax and incense returned.

Her son's voice returned. Zion.

"Mom! Mom! You're freaking me out! Do I need to call Brenda? An ambulance?" He sounded terrified. "Tell me what to do! Where's your phone?"

His voice was across the room then. She heard fumbling at her nightstand.

"No," she croaked out. "No phone. Just give me a minute."

She blinked. The room came into focus. She was lying on the floor, staring at the legs of her altar table. The right side of her head felt tender. She must have banged it when she fell.

She levered herself upright and leaned her back against the solid wood frame of her bed.

"Mom?"

"Come here, baby."

Zion sat down next to her. She wrapped her arms around his shoulders, pulling him close, and listened to him breathe.

It was enough for now, just to know that he was here, with her. But tomorrow?

"I'm sorry that my magic hasn't helped you. But we need to keep trying, okay? You have the amulet now. And I'll call those people about the martial arts."

She looked at his precious, battered face. "Okay?"

He nodded, solemnly.

"Okay, Mom."

"Love you, baby." Raquel kissed his forehead.

Get up, Raquel.

She staggered to her knees. Feeling like a failure as a mother and a witch, she was determined to find a way to help her son.

"Let's go make some dinner."

10

CHARLIE

Charlie's apartment was a one-bedroom above Owlbear, with multipaned warehouse windows, and wide-planked fir floors. The whole thing was painted white, a vestige from when he had leased the building. Before his father died and he became an actual property owner.

Maybe someday, Charlie would get around to adding color to the walls, but he had to get his dad's house cleared out and either put it up for sale or move in.

Charlie really felt at sea about that. He wasn't ready to deal with the weight of it all.

Original comic book art pages and framed posters added enough color to the apartment walls for now. All three lamps in his small living room were on, casting a warm light over the couch and bookcases crammed with graphic novels and art books as well as science fiction and noir mysteries.

Charlie sat in his favorite chair, a big, fake-leather cushioned rocker with a matching ottoman. He took a healthy swig of a slightly bitter, local IPA, straight from the bottle. Damn. All he'd wanted, after running game night, was to come home and chill.

Instead, he was staring down at the flier he'd ripped from the pole in front of Owlbear. A flier that no one in the shop knew shit about. No one had seen it go up, but Charlie *knew* it hadn't been there in the morning, when he opened the shop.

He'd been too distracted taking care of Zion that afternoon to have noticed if anything new had gone up on the streetlight pole when he walked the boy to Raquel's café.

No Blacks. No Muslims. No Mexicans. No Jews. The bold letters filled the sign, black on white. At the bottom, smaller letters read *KeepPortlandWhite.* The play on the Keep Portland Weird slogan made him want to punch something, or someone. If those damn white supremacist, HackMaster-playing assholes were behind it, they were in big trouble.

The men with the clean haircuts hadn't been at games night tonight, which was a good thing for them, because Charlie was spitting nails when he walked through the door, flier clutched in his right hand.

He was still angry, three hours later.

The beer was not doing its job of helping him to unwind.

All in all, game night had gone well, once Sam and a couple of his gaming buddies—mostly Jonathan and CJ— had gotten him calmed down. Along with the usual—a D&D campaign, a group of tweens playing Magic, and a rousing round of the Zelda board game—there was some interesting stuff going on.

Jonathan had helped run a game of Secret Hitler, which Charlie hadn't seen played before. The players were divided into two teams, Liberals and Fascists. The key was to try and stop the other side from taking over. The game was designed so it was remarkably hard to get the Liberals to side together long enough to stop the fascists from rolling through. No one knows who the fascists are, except other fascists. Nazis in progressive clothing.

Like the Nazis that had taped this sign in front of his shop. Racist, fascist sympathizers, who were nosing around his neighborhood and his business.

The book of runes he'd gotten from Brenda's shop was on the side table next to his chair. He took another swallow of beer, put the flier down, and opened the book.

"May as well learn something, instead of focusing on those assholes." Besides, Raquel's friend Brenda had told him he could use the symbols for protection.

"When people pervert the ancient symbols, one thing we can do is take them back, and use them to strengthen our position and ourselves. There are some good runes in there for strength and protection. And if you ever want to study them, and figure out what combinations work, we've got people in the coven who can help you, or we can introduce you to some heathens who aren't white supremacists." Brenda's words made sense to him.

Charlie wasn't sure he was ready to act on using the symbols yet, but figured the book was a good place to start. Know your enemy, and all that. And if he could protect Owlbear along with it? It was all to the good.

One thing about being a gamer, he knew the power of symbols to spark imagination. And imagination shifted people's thoughts and lives.

Fehu. The first rune looked like the letter F with its side bars tilted up. *Cattle. Sheep. Wealth.* Ancient people would have thought livestock were wealth. They were a lot more useful than gold, weren't they?

Charlie flipped through the book, looking for the letters that Brenda said might help. *Elhaz.* Which looked like a pitchfork. *Elk sedge. Boundary. Protection.* Right. This was the one Brenda had shown him.

He grabbed a small, spiral-bound notebook from the table, and wrote the rune down, making a note of its name.

There was the sound of breaking glass and a thump downstairs, then a *whoomf.*

"Shit!" Charlie threw the book down, set down his beer, and ran. Wrenching his apartment door open, he thundered down the outdoor stairs to the sidewalk, rounding the corner to the front of Owlbear.

A reddish-orange light danced through the windows. How big was it? Not too big. Yet.

Making a snap decision, he yanked his keys from his front pocket and opened the door, racing toward the large red fire extinguisher behind the counter. Hefting the weight of it, he pulled the pin, then aimed the nozzle at the base of the fire before squeezing the trigger.

Charlie coughed from the fumes. Acrid, oily smoke billowed out from the flames.

It smelled like kerosene. Like the stuff you used in tiki torches to light a late-night summer barbecue in your backyard.

Charlie stayed back as far as he could, sweeping the extinguisher back and forth. The flames licked upward, flaring and spitting. The foam blanketed the floor, starving the fire of oxygen until there was nothing left but smoke, foam, and a charred spot on the linoleum floor.

The smoke was terrible, but was already being sucked out through the broken window.

Charlie took his finger from the trigger, covered his mouth and nose with his elbow, and breathed, then coughed as the fumes hit him in a wave again. Still carrying the extinguisher, he walked back to the door, and yanked it open, stumbling out onto the sidewalk.

The chilly, late-April air felt good. He took in huge drafts of it, trying to clear the stinking smoke from his lungs. Looking down the sidewalk, he saw there wasn't much activity. The other nearby shops were all closed for the night, of course. A block away, a few people stood outside the brew pub. He'd have to ask if they saw anything.

But first, he supposed he should call the fire department. Make sure the thing was truly out. Charlie was wishing for his hoodie now, but didn't want to leave even long enough to run upstairs to get it.

Then something strange happened.

It felt as if a person had tapped the back of his head, right at the base of his skull where it met his spine. He paused for a moment, setting the extinguisher down on the sidewalk with a *chink*.

He was flooded with the certainty that the person he needed to call first was Raquel.

A sudden wind came up, and he shivered.

"Screw it," he said, and thumbed Raquel's contact up onto his phone. The weird, tapping sensation stopped.

As he waited for her to pick up, he jogged up the stairs to his apartment. Leaving his shop exposed for five minutes wasn't going to be the end of the world.

Besides, it was going to be a long night. He might as well be warm.

Nazis be damned.

11

RAQUEL

Raquel stumbled across the small grassy area to the sidewalk, and then up Brenda's walkway, smelling lavender and night blooming brugmansia, whose yellow-tinged trumpets hung down, blessing the rest of Brenda's front garden.

Slow your breathing down, dummy. Ground yourself! Raquel tried. Oh, she tried. But it still felt as if she rolled up Brenda's front steps like a wave. Giving two sharp raps to announce herself, she turned the knob and opened the door.

"Raquel!" Brenda leapt up from the goldenrod tapestry sofa and ran toward her. "Is everything all right? You said you weren't coming tonight!"

Raquel sank into her friend's fragrant embrace. Tuberoses. She wasn't all right. She was once again on the edge of panic, which was not the usual state for a single-parent, business-owning witch like Raquel. Raquel had her shit together. Raquel helped *train* people. Other people were the ones who freaked the shit out.

Not Raquel.

Not until now.

Leaning in to Brenda calmed her. Raquel was finally able to take in a breath that started from below her navel, instead of high up in her chest.

"Raquel?" Brenda voiced the question into her ear. Raquel nodded into her shoulder, then pulled away.

"Charlie called. Someone firebombed his shop."

"What?" Moss leapt to his feet, his wiry, muscular arms ending in clenched fists. Today's T-shirt showed cartoon sushi and read "That's How I Roll." His black hair stuck up in shocks around his head. "Do we need to go kick some butt?"

"Why don't we let Raquel tell us what's going on?" Lucy was the voice of reason for once. She could be as hotheaded as the next person, but had a practical streak. A Latinx housepainter, she was another successful businessperson. Arrow and Crescent was full of them.

Everyone was gathered in Brenda's living room. The walls were a paler shade of yellow, and the damask-covered chairs were a gorgeous sky blue. The fireplace was white brick. A painting of a woman with dusky skin, in Grecian-style robes and a peacock headdress, was hung, pride of place, over the mantel, flanked by paintings of the sun and the moon.

Raquel realized, even though she'd been alienated lately, Brenda's space still felt like home. And the faces of her coven staring at her, eyes big, still felt like family. Thank Goddess.

Raquel burst into tears.

"Okay," Brenda said. "Moss, since you're up, will you make Raquel tea? There should be a lavender mint infusion in one of the jars on the counter."

Arm still comfortingly around Raquel's waist, Brenda

gestured to Tobias, who was sitting forward in one of the damask chairs, worry creasing his face.

"Tobias, would you give Raquel your chair, please?"

"Oh!" He looked startled. "Of course!" He leapt up and held his arms open. Raquel gave him a quick hug. He smelled, as always, of whatever herbs and blends he'd been working with that day. The sharp, minty scent of pennyroyal mixed with the fiery scent of cayenne.

He moved past her then, and she sank into the chair, grateful for its soft embrace.

Tobias ducked into the kitchen to get another chair, coming back with Moss, who carried a mug of steaming tea.

"Thank you." She wiped her face, exhaled, and wrapped her hands around the heavy blue mug. Sure enough, lavender and mint. Hanging out with Arrow and Crescent was always a symphony of smells. It was part of how they knew one another, she supposed. Just like animals.

"So, are you going to tell us what happened?" Alejandro asked. His long fingers tapped impatiently on his navy trousers. Today's dress shirt was pale peach, warming up his pale brown skin.

"Sorry to fall apart like that," Raquel said. "But with Zion getting beat up, and the Nazi fliers everywhere...and now this? I'm feeling a little overwhelmed. And Yemoja came to me this evening. Pulled me down to the bottom of the damn ocean. I felt like I was drowning."

"But you aren't," Brenda said, voice gentle.

"But I'm not. She told me that, too. But I still *feel* like I am. And I feel ashamed of it," she admitted. "Doubting myself. Like I'm weak. I mean, I helped found this coven, right?"

"So that means you're never allowed to fall apart?"

Lucy's voice was dry as she handed Raquel a tissue. Always practical, Lucy was.

Raquel gave a little laugh, then blew her nose. "I freaked poor Zion out, though. He found me on the floor. I guess I was making noise or something. Goddess. This *never* happens to me."

"We get that, Raquel. And we love you. But if you don't tell us what the hell happened with Charlie..." Lucy's voice held a loving threat.

Raquel sipped the tea, letting the lavender and mint wash over her tongue, allowing the warmth to move all the way down through her body.

"What happened? After Zion picked me up off the floor, and I made us dinner, Charlie called. The only information I have is that he was upstairs, having a beer in his apartment, heard glass breaking, and then the shop was on fire. Luckily, it was a small one and he was able to contain it. Here's the thing, though... He called me before he called the fire department."

"And?" Alejandro prompted.

"He said something told him to call me. That 'your coven will know what to do,' is what he said. He's been finding fliers and Nazi writing around the shop. And he's worried about some dudes that have been gaming there lately."

"I sent him home with a book of runes," Brenda said. "I was hoping we'd have more time. But he's right, we can at least help with protecting the shop for now."

Raquel set the mug down on the wooden side table that sat between her chair and Alejandro's.

"He didn't exactly say it, but I could tell he wanted more than that. I mean, he mentioned the runes, and asked if

someone could help him set things up around Owlbear...
but that isn't why he was told to call me first."

"What are you thinking?" Lucy asked.

Raquel leveled a gaze at the housepainter. "I think you
know the answer to that. He was compelled to call me
because this isn't just about him, or his shop." She sighed,
still exhausted with it all. "The city needs more magical
help, and we seem to be the deputized guardians
these days."

"*That's* the truth," said Selene. They had eaten most of
their wine-colored lipstick off, and their face was even paler
than usual, set off by the black clothing that flowed down to
their tough-girl buckled boots. "We're going to need to talk
about that, by the way. We can't just let things keep happening, always on defense."

Raquel sat up, alarm bells ringing inside her heart. "Do
you mean we need to go on the offensive?"

Selene looked thoughtful, and picked up a slice of
cheese from the platter on the coffee table in the center of
the cluster of chairs.

"Not exactly," they said. "But, come on. Here we were,
gaily planning our Beltane ritual, and you bust in, with
trouble following you. This is happening all the time now.
Once every cross quarter, at least. So, what is the universe
trying to tell us?"

"That gaily planning rituals is badass?" Tobias quipped.
Moss threw a cloth napkin at him. It fluttered to the ground
before it reached Tobias's lap.

"Sorry. I know as much as anyone that this is serious."

Tobias—and his now-boyfriend Aiden—were at the
center of the magical and political maelstrom the coven had
been involved with at Imbolc, the holiday on the cusp of

February. And the coven had dealt with another threat since.

Raquel waved those thoughts away. Her head knew all of that. So did her heart. But Selene was right. What was being asked of Arrow and Crescent?

And what was being asked of *her*? This fight had come directly to her door, when she was feeling at her weakest. It brought threats to her son, and now threats to the man who was trying to help him.

A man that Raquel had to admit she was attracted to. Every person had a task. Raquel was a firm believer in that. She used to know what hers was. First, she loved and protected her son. That still stood. Second, she provided a safe place for community to gather. Third? She served her Goddesses and Gods. Lately, she had more and more trouble with those last two.

And now something else was banging on her door. She had been charged by Yemoja to live in her power. To claim it again. What did that look like? She knew what it *didn't* look like. It sure as Goddess didn't look like waiting for the fight to show up at your door. Damn. She didn't want this.

She just wanted a normal, happy life.

"We need to plan," Lucy said. "We need to train. Selene is right. We can't just react all the time. We're being called upon to *act*."

"But what does that look like?" Tobias asked.

Lucy leaned forward, eyes intense. "It looks like getting serious about self-defense, for ourselves and our communities. It looks like setting up magical systems to stop this shit before it starts, as often as we can."

"I still don't understand," Tobias said. "I mean, I get that on a basic, spiritual level, but what's it look like in real time?"

Raquel sat back in the damask chair again, and picked up her tea.

"I think that's what we need to figure out," she said. "And I don't think we're going to comprehend it right away."

Raquel looked to Brenda, waiting for her best friend, the woman whom she'd founded this coven with, to speak. She had her eyes closed, listening to something not on the physical plane. Her palms lay, face up, on her thighs.

"Brenda?"

She opened her blue eyes. Blinked a few times.

"Selene is right, and so are you, and Lucy. This is a big thing we're being tasked with, and we're not going to figure it out in the next month, or even a quarter. But we need to start asking. We need to do divination. We need to listen. Deeply. And we need to look at all the ways we've been avoiding this, as a coven, and in our own lives."

A shiver crawled up Raquel's spine. Too close to home.

"Damn, girlfriend. You know how to make a person feel good about themselves," Raquel said.

Brenda laughed, and the heaviness in the living room shattered into a thousand pieces.

"While we start to figure out what to do for Charlie, though, can we open a bottle of wine?" Raquel said.

"I think that's just the thing," Brenda replied. She rose, and kissed Raquel's forehead.

One glass of wine, a little more conversation, and then Raquel needed to pick Zion up from her neighbor's house, and get the poor boy to bed, then crawl into bed herself.

This was all too much.

:But you have the strength to handle it.: said a voice inside her head.

"Thanks, Yemoja," Raquel murmured.

She just wished she believed it.

12

CHARLIE

The hiss of the cappuccino maker filled the air, a counterpoint to the bouncy Bruno Mars song piped over the general hum of conversation.

Moss, Raquel's—coven mate?—had suggested they meet up at Raquel's café for breakfast. Charlie had no idea what to call the wiry Asian guy who had offered to help him learn runes. He was younger than both Raquel and Charlie, looked to be in his mid-twenties.

The guy was filled with energy, practically bouncing in his chair, pen tapping on the notebook opened on the table in front of him as he thought. No wonder the guy was so skinny and strong. He probably burned off a million calories just watching television.

The scent of coffee mingled with the odor of grilled bread, bacon, and cheese.

Charlie's stomach rumbled. He was wishing he'd gotten a breakfast panini instead of just one of Raquel's signature red ceramic cups of coffee. The place was busy, and so was Raquel, which was just as well, because, damn, Charlie found her distracting. If she had time to spend on him, he wouldn't be able to pay attention to Moss at all. Even in the red apron that covered up the front of her, he had a hard time not staring at her luscious curves and full, deep brown lips. Lips that he was dying to taste.

"Earth to Charlie. Come in, Charlie." Moss rapped on the tabletop. Charlie snapped back to attention, seeing the young man staring at him, a slight smirk on his face. There was now a strange combination of lines inscribed on the notebook page.

"I get it, Raquel is hot, but I don't have all day to work on this stuff while you moon over my coven mate."

Charlie felt a blush creeping up his neck. Well, at least he got that one question answered. Coven mate was a phrase.

"Sorry." He gulped down some cooling coffee and gestured to the notebook. "So, you were saying something about making combinations of runes or something?"

"They're called bindrunes. They're a form of sigil that people make for protection, prosperity, love, luck...whatever they need. You know what a sigil is, right?"

"I could hardly call myself a gamer if I didn't," Charlie replied.

Moss swung the notebook around so it was facing Charlie. "See this series of lines that looks like an upside down U?" He traced the shape with his finger. "That's the letter uruz, which represents the aurochs, wild cattle that are now extinct. It's commonly used to invoke strength and physical power. I've drawn that out in a mirror image, and extended the center line upward."

Moss traced the central shape, a capital Y with the cross bar reaching upward in the middle. Charlie recognized that shape.

"That's the rune for protection, right? I was looking at

that when my shop burst into flames." He grimaced at the memory, staring down at the paper. The lines seemed to move, shimmering on the page, as though the bold pen strokes were embossed. Charlie shook his head. Must need more coffee.

Moss continued. "So, the mirrored uruz runes, combined with elhaz, that central rune, also form a third rune." His pale brown finger traced a capital M shape. "That's ehwaz, the horse and rider, working in harmony. The rune of partnership. So between the three runes, we have strength and protection working together in balance. You can also read this combination as working with another person, or group of people, in a strong partnership that is going to protect you all."

The tapping sensation was back at the base of Charlie's skull. He slid a hand beneath the fall of blond hair that he'd worn loose today, and massaged the area. It felt warm to the touch. Then his forehead began buzzing, and his eyes lost focus for a moment.

The café dimmed and blurred around him. He could still hear that Moss was speaking, and music was playing, but the sounds were muted, as if he were listening to something underwater.

Then sound and sight snapped back into focus. Charlie's stomach lurched with vertigo.

"You okay, man?" Moss had a crease between his black eyebrows.

"Um. Yeah. Things got a little wonky there for a minute."

"Wonky how?"

Charlie shrugged. How the hell was he going to explain what had happened to this guy he barely knew? He didn't even know how to explain it to himself.

Moss shifted in his chair, until he was sitting canted, one

leg crossed, foot over his knee. He drank his coffee, continuing to stare at Charlie, while giving him some time to collect himself. Then his foot began to shake, whether with impatience or just that boundless energy of his, Charlie wasn't sure. He just knew it wasn't helping his own nerves any. The words were definitely not coming.

Finally, Moss set the red ceramic cup down and leaned forward.

"I'm a witch, man. I'm used to all kinds of strange shit. Besides, I'm here to help you. I can't help you if you don't tell me what's up."

Charlie cleared his throat and rolled his shoulders, trying to ease the tension that gripped his torso. "The runes moved."

Moss grew still, as if he was listening with his whole body. "Moved how?"

"Um...they started to shimmer? Then looked like they were raised on the page."

Moss tapped his lips with the pen. "Interesting. They still look that way?"

Charlie looked down at the paper. The symbols were inert again. Still. He shook his head.

"Did anything else happen?"

Charlie reached for the words again. "Yeah. It was as if the café receded. Like I was underwater. Or the café was."

"And you've never worked with runes before?"

"No."

Moss tapped the paper for a moment, then flipped to a blank sheet. He scratched a shape on the white page. It looked like a spear, pointing up.

"What happens when you look at this?"

As Charlie looked down, he realized he was holding his breath. Nerves. Shaking himself, he tried to relax and breathe normally. He looked again. Felt the muscles in his back and shoulders engage, as if he was about to do pull downs, or a lat press at the gym.

"My spine feels supported by my muscles."

"That's good. But no weirdness in the café?"

Charlie shook his head.

Moss drew another shape. This one looked like a line with half a diamond sticking out of the middle. The lines darkened and grew thick. The shape grew larger on the page. A roaring started in Charlie's head. The base of his skull throbbed; his brow tingled. The shape grew and grew until it obliterated his view of Moss, of the café...of everything. It was all that he could see. Or feel. Or sense. Then it slammed into him, jerking him backwards, but he didn't fall.

He felt stronger than he had in a long time. Certain. True.

As though his whole life had just changed shape.

Charlie's muscles felt pumped, the way they did after a workout. His abs and lower back supported him. His shoulders felt as if he could support the world.

The café was back. The music had changed to some old Bowie. Moss's gaze was steady. Measuring him. Assessing him.

Charlie was suddenly ravenous, his earlier mild hunger had roared into full on need. He looked around to see if there was a line at the counter. And saw her. Raquel. She was luminous. Glowing around the edges. Strong. Soft. Alive. He was hungry for her, too. He wanted her like he'd never wanted anyone before.

And she stared at him as if she felt the same, rooted to the spot, mouth half open.

There was no line at the counter.

There was just her. And all of a sudden she was walking

toward their table, moving through the café as if she were swimming through clear water.

"What happened?" she asked. Coffee and mint. Plus the warm smell that must be her skin. And...cocoa butter? Something delicious.

"Turns out your man here has a strong affinity for the runes," Moss said. "And I do believe he's just been claimed by Thor."

A laugh burst from Charlie's chest. "You have to be kidding me, right? Just because everyone says I look like Chris Hemsworth..."

Moss and Raquel were both shaking their heads.

"It's not that," Raquel said. "I felt something change. And it felt big. Like a God."

Moss looked at Raquel. "The runes started speaking to him. Changing shape. And when I drew the rune thurisaz, all of a sudden *he* changed."

What did that even mean? Charlie looked from Moss to Raquel.

She swept her gaze around his body, as if she could see some strangeness surrounding him. With a sharp nod, her eyes came back into focus. It was uncomfortable, the way she looked at him.

He felt exposed. She knew too much. Saw too much. He'd never had a woman look at him that way before. Never let them.

"What do you see?" he finally asked.

"Moss is right. I see runes all around you, and you're definitely God-touched now. Where are your ancestors from?"

Charlie shrugged. "I'm a mutt, like most Americans. Some Swedish. Some English. And my dad's father was from Germany."

"Well, fuck," Moss said.

"Is that bad?"

Raquel bit the inside of her lip, just for a second, and crossed her arms over her chest.

"It's not bad…" she said. "Actually, it might be good. It might be just what we need to fight those Nazi assholes."

"I don't understand."

"You can fight them power to power, as equals. Blood and ancestry aren't everything, that's for sure. I mean, look at me. A Japanese American dude who works with runes," Moss said. "But since we know these assholes are tapping their bloodline and perverting the runes with it, we can leverage your ancestry to counteract them. Head them off at the pass."

Charlie sat back in his chair. "Okay. I'm going to need a lot more explanation than this, but I'm willing to go with it for now. But first, I need a mountain of food."

Raquel smiled down at him. His heart flipped. "That's pretty common after magical work. And luckily, you're in a place that makes some of the best sandwiches in town."

Charlie smiled back, but he felt troubled.

He wondered if this had anything to do with his dad.

And his dad's friends.

13

RAQUEL

Raquel and Zion stood in the small park adjacent to the community center, towering pines rising above them, creating a canopy of needles and branches that framed the day's blue sky.

The air was fresh and slightly chilly, scented with grass and pine, and the warm boy scent of her son. It was a beautiful day. Raquel should have been happy and relaxed.

As if.

Her hand was on Zion's shoulder. She knew he was allowing it under sufferance. Though still affectionate at home, it was a bit much to ask a thirteen-year-old to stand this close to his mother in public. Especially in front of the group of strong, agile men and women sparring in a clearing near the baseball field.

But she couldn't bear to have Zion far from her right now. Not while his face was still bruised and slightly puffy. Not while those damn white boys were out there. Despite the charged medallion around his neck, Raquel wasn't trusting him to the ancestors' protection yet.

The boy needed his mother.

The good thing about owning a café was having staff who could take care of the four o'clock closing when Raquel had errands to run.

Or needed to pick up Zion after school to meet with some people she wasn't yet certain of. People, about a half dozen of them, doing the strange and beautiful martial dances on the grass, dressed in black sweat pants with white or red shirts.

White and red. The colors of Changó. Ṣàngó. Xangô. A spirit of lightning. A spirit of war. A being she, as a witch, would call a God, but what others would call a Power, a spirit, an emissary.

She'd spent part of her morning doing research and making phone calls. Zion wanted self-defense lessons and was going to get them. She just hoped this group was the right one.

Always back up the spiritual with the physical was one magical tenet Raquel adhered to. *Work on all the planes of existence* was a more fancy way of putting it. So, prayers, offerings, and protective medals were about to be joined by learning to kick, punch, and stand tall.

The group was a mixture of ages, from mid-twenties to firmly middle-aged. Five Black men, one Asian woman, and a white guy. Seven people, then. Their fists snapped out, blocked by open palms. Legs swept out in kicks that tumbled opponents to the ground. She could hear hisses and grunts, and the occasional groan or bark of laughter.

"Want to go closer?" she asked Zion.

His eyes trained on the practicing warriors, Zion nodded. Looking down at his battered face caused her stomach muscles to clench. Her baby boy.

Not a baby anymore.

"Let's go."

She removed her hand from his shoulder and they walked across the grass. The group had broken up. A couple of people were drinking from metal water bottles, another few seemed to be discussing technique. She walked toward the two men who were taking weapons out of long black duffle bags.

She knew they worked with weapons. The website had said so. Nonetheless, the sight of blunted blades and long wooden sticks scared her, just a little.

:This is necessary. Have no fear. These men will show the way.:

Thank you, mother.

Raquel was slowly getting used to Yemoja speaking inside her head. And right now? She needed it. Times had been so confusing lately that clear guidance came as a welcome relief.

One of the men looked up as they approached. He wore a black knit cap that stuck out in back, clearly covering a large coil of dreadlocks. His dark face wore a light sheen of sweat. His cheekbones were high, ending in round knobs. Despite the chill in the air, he'd abandoned his red sweatshirt at some point, and wore only a red tank shirt, revealing muscled arms.

The shirt read "Sons of Ṣàngó" in white letters.

"Greetings, sister. Are you Raquel?"

He stood, wiping his hands on black cargo pants before extending it out. They shook. His hand was firm. A man she could respect. Handsome, too.

"I am. And this is Zion."

"Greetings, brother." He shook Zion's hand with a smile. "My name is Shawn, and that other brother is Seye."

The name was pronounced in the Yoruba way: *shay-ye.*

The other man was much larger than Shawn, a white T-shirt straining across his broad chest and solid belly. His shirt read "Sons of Ṣàngó" in red. Two handsome Black men, sons of Ṣàngó, indeed. She just hoped she could entrust her son to their care. And to the care of Ṣàngó's fire and lightning.

:*Trust.*:

"I trust you," she blurted. Oh, Goddess. The men looked at her, startled, then burst out laughing.

"Spirits talking to you, are they?" Seye said.

She grinned and shook her head. "Like they do, right? You'll be glad to know that Yemọja is on your side."

"We always welcome our mother's blessing," Shawn said. "I thought I saw her around you."

Wow. She was standing in a Portland park talking about the Powers with two Black men.

"How have we never met before?" she asked. It really made no sense. The Black community in Portland was not very large.

"I was raised in Salem," Shawn replied, "but only moved back to the area from Atlanta last year. Six months ago, I convinced Seye to come with me."

"Don't get me wrong, I love Portland, but can't imagine leaving a Black mecca like Atlanta to live here," Raquel said.

"Couldn't handle the humidity. And I missed these mountains and trees."

"Now that I can understand. But what about you?" she asked the large, shaved-headed man.

"I go where Ṣàngó tells me I'm needed. And it seems like things are heating up here, you know?"

Raquel exhaled. That was the unfortunate truth. And she knew the way the Powers worked. They made sure the right people were in place at the right time, whenever possible. But these men showing up in Portland when the racists were growing bold again? It wasn't good.

"I just hope things don't get as bad as they were in the late eighties," she said.

Seye pressed his lips together and shrugged. The message was clear: things were bad and only about to get worse.

Damn.

"You ready for me to show you some moves, young man?" Shawn asked Zion.

Zion nodded.

"Okay. Seye, will you get the rest of the group started on the weapons while I give young Zion some instruction?"

"Sure thing."

Shawn knelt next to Zion, looking him up and down. "How much training have you had?"

"Nothing."

"Huh. Really? You seem like you've had some training."

Her son looked at her then, as though asking her permission to speak.

She nodded. "Go ahead. You can tell him."

Zion looked down, digging at the grass with the toe of his sneaker. She saw when he changed, coming to an internal decision. His shoulders straightened and he raised his head.

"I know some magic," he said, looking at Shawn dead-on.

If the man was surprised, he didn't show it. Raquel had to respect him for that.

"Well, then. That's good. Magic is a powerful thing. We don't practice magic, but we respect it. You honor your ancestors?" he asked.

Zion nodded. "Yeah."

"We've just upped our practice, as a matter of fact," Raquel said. "After *that* happened."

She gestured to Zion's face.

Shawn looked serious. "We will teach you how to handle yourself with bullies, and how to head them off before they get that close again. Sound good?"

"Sounds good."

Shawn stood and addressed her then.

"Okay, woman of Yemoja, if you are willing, we will get Zion started. Just a short session today. Can you come back in thirty minutes?"

"Oh! I thought...yes. Of course." She'd thought she would stay and watch, but Yemoja had told her to trust these men, and so she would. She turned to Zion. Her beautiful boy. He looked up at her, and she saw that, behind the bruises and scrapes, his eyes looked sure.

"I'll see you soon, Zion."

"See you, mom."

Then she forced herself to turn and walk away.

14

CHARLIE

The shop was quiet, which was strange for early afternoon. Charlie looked around Owlbear, eyes scanning the walls of games, the display cases of figurines, the collectibles, the empty gaming tables in the back.

His domain. His home. The ground he stood on, ready to battle orcs, twisted wizards, or white men bent on bullying and hate.

He felt equal parts freaked out by what had happened at Raquel's café that morning, and excited at the power he had felt.

He'd spent a good portion of the night before with the rune book opened in front of him, studying the symbols. This morning, Moss had told him that when he was ready to activate a rune, it should be drawn in red. After some hesitation, Raquel's coven mate had admitted that the proper way to charge a rune was with the practitioner's blood.

"But I don't think you're ready for that kind of commitment, yet. You need to form a relationship with the runes first. Get to know them. Let the alphabet get to know you."

"You act as if they're alive," Charlie had said.

Raquel and Moss had both laughed out loud at that.

"After what you just experienced, you doubt that?" Raquel had asked. He'd flushed at that. Flushed now, remembering. He had wanted to kiss her so badly in that moment. All of a sudden, his body was responding to her as more than just the attractive woman who owned his neighborhood café.

"Focus, Charlie," he muttered to himself.

It was true that he wanted more from Raquel, and hoped she was interested in exploring that. It seemed so, because before he left the café, he'd gotten an agreement for a date that night. At least, he would if Raquel could get her mother or a friend to babysit Zion for a few hours.

So that was good. He'd finally get to kiss those full lips. Hope fluttered behind his tight stomach muscles.

But enough of that. For now, it seemed as if the runes wanted more from him, too. And he really wanted to get some protections up around the shop. The place had to be safe for the children who considered Owlbear a haven. If an ancient alphabet had any chance of helping, he was going to take the foolish risk and try.

With a roll of red electrician's tape in his hand, Charlie looked for good places to tuck some runes. Eventually, he would paint them on the walls, and yeah, maybe even add a drop or two of his blood to the paint, though the jury was still out on that last part. But for now, he would just feel better having the runes up on the walls.

The Charlie of three months ago would have raised an eyebrow at thinking runes could offer any protection other than during a dungeon crawl. But shit was getting real, wasn't it?

If the magic he'd spent his life playing fantasy games with turned out to be real, he might need to re-evaluate his world view. For now, Charlie figured that if magic existed, the world needed the kind of magic people like Raquel and Moss worked with. It couldn't hurt. Right?

So he was keeping an open mind. Might as well perform some tests and see what the results were, dusting off the old scientific method he'd studied in high school.

Besides, he couldn't shake the feeling he'd gotten of pure power coursing through his body. The feeling that Moss and Raquel had both said was linked to Thor.

"Fuck." He didn't know if he wanted to call that sense of power *Thor*, like Moss and Raquel had, but there was no denying it wasn't exactly Charlie-flavored. He could ponder all of that later. Or not.

Charlie found a blank patch of wall not covered by shelves, displays, or posters, planted his feet, and took a breath, just the way Moss had suggested. Then he glanced down at the bindrunes he and Moss had worked with the day before one more time. Taking another breath, he unrolled the tape into the pattern, cutting the ends with scissors as he went, so the edges would be sharp. Defined.

The first shapes appeared on the wall. Mirrored, downward facing, angular u shapes. Uruz. The wild aurochs. Strength. Then the central post, up between the two, which formed the bifurcated Y. Elhaz. The sharp blades of elk sedge. Protection. Boundary.

Charlie stepped back a moment, to make certain the angles looked right. His eyes traced the red lines on the stark, white patch of wall. Three shapes were present, just as Moss had designed. Strength. Protection. Partnership. Uruz. Elhaz. Ehwaz.

He filled his lungs with another breath, and held out his right hand to touch the rune. As he exhaled, Charlie felt a tingling on his palm, spreading to his fingertips. He imagined that tingling entering the shape of the bindrune.

"You need to link your power to the power of the symbol for it to work," Moss had told him.

Charlie closed his eyes, imagining every nerdy kid who had ever walked through his door. He imagined the middle-aged gamers, recapturing some of the joy they'd had when they were younger, before life had beaten them down. He imaged boys, girls, teens, women, men, and the non-binary crew that were regulars at game nights.

"Owlbear is a place of safety and community for all of these people," Charlie said out loud to the empty shop.

He swore he felt the rune shape pulse once beneath his hand. Then all was quiet. Gently, he lifted his hand from the wall, and looked at his palm. Nothing looked different.

But he *felt* different, all the same. No time to ponder it, though. There was work to be done.

He queued up his favorite Swiss folk-metal, a band called Eluveitie, and started combing through the notes Sam had left him from yesterday's closing, along with the overall numbers. Looked like Owlbear was having a good week, overall.

The *Star Trek* phaser noise sounded, and Charlie looked up. It was two of the white men he'd been keeping an eye on. The HackMaster dudes with the matching floppy-topped, high-and-tight haircuts.

He nodded to the men. "Good morning."

"I like the music today, man," said the one on the right. His hair was dark, sharp face outlined in a fashionable dusting of stubble. He wore a close-fitting black jacket with a reversed black-and-gray-scale American flag on the shoulder.

His friend, a blond, was dressed in a navy blazer over

skinny jeans and loafers with no socks. No socks in the Pacific Northwest before June? Either vanity or stupidity. Maybe a combination of both.

Charlie's stomach clenched and the aftertaste of his morning's cup of coffee soured in his mouth. Damn. He really didn't want to deal with these dudes. He stood a little taller. Imagined the protective rune he had just placed on the far wall. A small trickle of the power he'd felt that morning flowed into his veins, and along the edges of his skin.

Thanks, Thor, he thought. *Or whoever you are.*

"Let me know if you need anything."

Dark-haired dude stopped. Right in front of the bindrune Charlie had just put up. He whirled his head around and shot Charlie a wolfish grin.

Damn. Charlie would have to ask Moss about cloaking the thing. This was not what was supposed to happen.

"Runes, huh? The Reichsadler." The man's grin broadened as he spoke the German word. Charlie filed the sounds away to look up later. He rolled his shoulders back and stepped toward the two men.

"They're here to protect the shop. To protect everyone who walks through the door. Except for Nazi assholes. They're meant to repel those."

Blond-haired, no-socks stepped forward. "Hey, man. Watch your mouth. We thought you were coming around." The man looked Charlie up and down. "You're one of us, man. Why don't you just admit it? I know your father's friends. They all agree with me."

Charlie's blood chilled. His father's friends. His father's fucking friends. That was a little confirmation he didn't need right now.

"Besides," said Dark Hair, "we've got no problem with

non-white people. We just think everyone is stronger when they stick with their own culture. Right? Native Americans have Native stuff. Caribbean people have Caribbean stuff."

"And gamer geeks? Nerds? Do they come in some particular race?" Charlie's jaw was so tight, it was a miracle he could get the words out. "Get the fuck out of my shop."

Both men's faces shuttered at that, mouths settling in tight lines.

"You're making a mistake, my friend," said Blond No Socks.

Dark Hair shoved the door open. As the phaser sounded, he shouted out "White Pride!"

His blond friend followed, sweeping a hand across the counter, sending baskets of nerdy pins, small decks of playing cards, and the display of keychain ray guns bouncing to the floor.

"We'll be back, loser," the blond man said, without even a glance back.

Charlie exhaled and unclenched his fists.

Then he bent to clean up the mess.

15

RAQUEL

They were in Roscoe's, the dance club downtown. The amber lights were moody, and warmed the wooden sweep of the bar, reflecting off glass bottles and highlighting people's cheekbones and lips. The music was jamming, and there was a decent amount of people stalking each other across the decent-sized dance floor. They'd found an empty little standing two top table, only large enough for her small purse and drinks when they got them. It had a decent view of the bar and the dancers.

Raquel really could not remember the last time she'd been out dancing. But it turned out Zion had a homework-and-movie date after dinner. She'd just forgotten about it, what with everything else happening. He was so excited she had an "actual date," he practically bounced as he bounded out the door to his ride.

Zion really like Charlie. Raquel shook her head slightly. She was going to have to watch out for that. It wouldn't do for Zion to get attached to this man, and have things fall through.

At least he had loved working with the Sons of Ṣàngó.

He'd walked a little taller after the practice than when she'd left him at the park. They'd discussed a training schedule, and would have to figure out how he was getting there after school three days a week. The group leader, Shawn, had given her a respectful little half bow as they left, but there was a little heat in his eyes, too.

She had to admit that was nice. And if it weren't for whatever in Goddess's name she was feeling with Charlie, she would have definitely been interested.

Raquel hadn't been affected by a man like this in years. Really, despite her prayers to the contrary, she still wondered if she even had time for it. She had a business to run and employees to take care of. Plus, ever since Andy was killed by an IED in Afghanistan, she was raising a child on her own.

She had love aplenty. Raquel had the coven, she had Brenda, and Zion…. She was offered more love than she ever thought was possible, even though it didn't always feel like family. Not like having your one person to rely on. The way other people had.

Since Brenda and Caroline had gotten together, Raquel had been feeling a little…forlorn. She was happy for her friend, but missed her. Some of the closeness they'd had was at least temporarily gone.

And romance? Romance was another animal entirely. She hadn't had romance in forever. Charlie smelled so good. He smelled of blackboard chalk and sunlight. A strange combination maybe, but it did her in.

"You want a drink?" Charlie asked.

She stopped her woolgathering with a shake of her head.

"That shake of your head mean no? Or is something

bothering you? You've shaken your head a couple of times since we walked through the door."

"Oh, sorry, no. I mean yes." She smiled up at him. "I would like a drink, thank you. Martini, dry, extra olive." She avoided the other questions and, thankfully, all he did was pause for a moment, waiting, before brushing a hand across her shoulder and smiling.

"Sure thing," he said, then pushed his way through the crowd the bar. She watched him go. His usual T-shirt had been replaced by a long-sleeved pale blue shirt with diamond shapes woven in the cloth. His broad shoulders filled out the pale blue shirt, tapering to hips that were slim, but not so slender that he didn't still have a terrific ass beneath his black jeans.

Raquel pulled her eyes away and looked out over the dance floor. It was R&B night. She loved to dance to R&B. She had to admit, it felt nice being in a dress and two-inch heels for once, instead of boots or sneakers and jeans.

More Black people filled the club than she usually saw in any one Portland place. Probably because of the music. Sometimes she'd go out to an event, and it seemed as if every Black person in Portland was there in attendance. She gave a few people a nod and a smile. That felt good too. Not only to be out, but to be out somewhere where it wasn't just a sea of white faces. You'd think having been born and raised in Portland, Raquel would be used to it. Mostly she was, until she ended up someplace like this, and saw how life must be for people in Baltimore or Oakland.

Yemọja. *Goddess. Mother ocean... What do you want from my heart? Why have you brought this particular man into my life? Is he the one I've been wanting?*

She was certain it was the Goddess who had done this. It

all started after Zion gifted her with that piece of sea glass on the Oregon coast. She had prayed for love, hadn't she? She could barely remember. It'd only been a few days in reality, but it felt like a lifetime. The Goddess didn't answer her, but Raquel saw Charlie making his way back to her, her martini in one large hand, and what looked like a bourbon and soda in the other. A huge, stupid smile split his beautiful face. She saw heads snap around to stare at him as he walked. No denying, the man was gorgeous, even if he was a goofy nerd.

Chris Hemsworth, eat your heart out.

"Here you are, beautiful." He raised his glass and looked at her expectantly. "Toast?"

Raquel closed her eyes and took a breath. What did she want to toast to? Toasts were serious things to witches, even the lighthearted ones. Sharing a toast was sharing a spell with somebody.

:To strong hearts and open minds.: The Goddess's voice rang in her head.

Raquel steeled herself, planted her feet and their fancy shoes on the floor beneath her, took in a breath. *Time to take a risk, girl.*

"To possibility," she said.

"Possibility," he replied, touching the rim of his glass to hers.

You chickened out, she thought. Well, she couldn't be brave all the time. Besides, believing in possibility with this man was going to require both a strong heart *and* an open mind. She hoped she was up for it, because right now, all she wanted to do was kiss this man.

Instead, she took a drink. It was crisp and cold with just a hint of vermouth to temper the gin.

"So, how was your day?"

He grimaced at that. "Had to throw a couple of Nazi asshats out of the shop."

"Really?" She chilled at that. "They seem to be everywhere, these days."

Charlie took a sip of his bourbon and soda and nodded. "They are. And we should definitely talk about it, in case the café becomes a target, too. But tonight? I really just want to have a drink and dance with you."

She took two sips of her martini in quick succession, then set her glass down.

Lips still wet with alcohol, she leaned forward. He leaned, too. Their lips met. Warm. Soft. Firm. Delicious.

When he pulled away from her, it felt like the ocean receding. She wanted to pull him back.

"Let's dance," Charlie said, putting his drink down. He held out a hand, and she tucked one of hers inside. Then he pulled her onto the dance floor.

So tall. Broad. Raquel wasn't a small woman, but he still towered over her. He wore no tie, so the shirt collar framed his neck, the color lighting up his eyes.

Eyes that looked at her with desire.

Oh Goddess. What in the world was she doing? She hadn't...

:You are a woman. It is time.:

So, Yemoja was giving sex and love advice now? Raquel smiled. Of course she was. As a witch, Raquel knew that sex was one powerful way to move life force, and the energy that fueled every living thing was stock in trade for a priestess.

And, as Raquel was not asexual, or even demisexual, it made sense that she should channel life force in one of its more obvious forms.

Through dance, of course. But yeah, the vee between her thighs was pulsing, reminding her that she needed sex, too.

Those of us who enjoy sex only honor the Gods by engaging in consensual sexual activity. That was one of the tenets of the coven. Arrow and Crescent acknowledged that not everyone enjoyed sex, but those who did? There was no shame in it. It was a sacred act, always. Whether a casual hookup or sex between people who were in long-term commitments.

All of this flickered through Raquel's mind in the space of thirty seconds. During that time, her body had taken control, moving and swaying to the music, which had shifted from rhythm and blues and into some Afro-Latinx beats. Her feet were moving, front to back. Her hips swayed and snapped.

She was dancing toward Charlie, and then away. Enticing. Testing. Seeing if he would respond.

His movements matched hers. Hips followed feet. Hands reached out and back. She could feel the edges of his hands, tracing her aura. She felt their energy fields bumping against one another, penetrating, then moving out again. But never too far away.

Oh, yes. Charlie could dance. And her body clearly wanted to dance with him.

His usually pale brown eyes looked dark in the night-club light. They never left her face.

Charlie leaned in closer. She could smell the warmth of his skin, and had to stop herself from grabbing him by the neck and pulling him closer still.

"You are so gorgeous, Raquel. Amazing."

Then he leaned away again, and their bodies continued the circling dance.

The music increased its tempo. Raquel stomped her feet, then threw back her head and laughed. Charlie laughed with her.

Goddess. It was so good.

Finally, the beat dropped back down, and the DJ segued cleanly back into a slow, sexy R&B song. Aloe Blacc, singing about facing the sun.

Charlie's hands slid around Raquel's hips, drawing her closer. Her hands glided up his chest, coming to rest on either side of his neck.

"Charlie?" she said.

He lowered his head, until his lips were near her right ear.

"I want to kiss you."

"That's good," he replied, and moved his face just enough to look into her eyes.

They pressed their mouths together, and danced some more. That swaying, rocking, dance whose only beat was "more."

16

CHARLIE

The shop buzzed with after-school activity. Sam had just come on shift. She was running game night. Groups of kids squealed over toys and conferred in excited tones over the latest shipment of games, or did who knew what back at the gaming tables.

Charlie had just finished telling Sam and Hai about the visitation from the Nazis the day before.

Hai had just arrived. He'd been in the neighborhood checking out a comic book collection. The woman who owned them had been a major collector before cancer took its toll. Charlie had texted him the night before, letting him know about the minor fracas in the shop. Hai replied immediately that he'd be in the neighborhood and would stop by.

"They mentioned a *reichsadler*. Ever heard of that?" Charlie asked.

They clustered around the long glass counter, where Sam and Charlie could keep an eye on the store. Hai leaned against the glass, one sneakered foot resting on the other. Charlie never understood how people could stand that way.

He'd studied too much martial arts in his day to not have his feet stable, ready to move in a moment.

"The Imperial Eagle," Hai replied, voice tight. "You know it. The Germans stole it from Rome. The Nazis gave it a swastika to clutch in its talons."

Of course. Charlie wasn't a history or war gamer, so the name hadn't clicked right away. But he could picture it now. A great black eagle with outstretched wings.

Sam was so pissed off, she practically vibrated, arms crossed over her chest so you could barely see the black-and-white gaming dice forming a yin-yang symbol on her T-shirt. Her fingers tapped at her arms. Sam's long black hair was braided and slicked back from her face, which bristled with two extra piercings—when had she gotten those?—and her mouth was set in a scowl.

Hai was angry, too, though he was being less extreme about it. His gamer-geek cool cred was intact, barely. Both of them stared Charlie down.

"Look, guys, it's going to be okay," Charlie said. "Those HackMaster Nazis won't be back."

Charlie kept his voice low. He didn't want to alarm the two groups of pre-teens excitedly scanning the game shelves and the barely teens having a spirited argument about who-knew-what back at the gaming tables. Zion was part of that group, face still bruised, though his busted lip was looking slightly better.

Hai shook his head.

"I think you're wrong, my friend, following on the heels of the fire? You just got the glass replaced, man." Hai raked fingers through his dark shock of hair. "Sam is right to be pissed. Those dudes hate people like us, and think they own the world. As long as they're allowed in here, it really isn't safe. Frankly, the whole neighborhood's at risk."

Hai looked around, scanning the store. "I mean, look at these kids. Look at me and Sam. You think the world is comfortable for people who look like us? Being a nerd is bad enough, and then *Portland* is bad enough, without having to wade through Nazis at our favorite places."

"We're supposed to be a *haven*, Charlie," Sam spat out.

Charlie threw up his hands, and leaned toward her. The cords on his neck stood out from the effort to keep his voice soft. He wanted to shout.

"That's what I've been trying to *do*, Sam. What, am I the enemy now, because some assholes have been coming into the shop?"

She exhaled in a huff. "Owlbear has to take a stronger stance, Charlie. You know that."

"Kicking those dudes out today wasn't enough?"

She just shook her head at that and looked at the red tape on the wall. "And the runes? Seriously? How is that good?"

"They were supposed to help protect the shop. You know, use their magic powers against them." At least that was the theory. But he felt a little stupid about it all now. Maybe he should have waited until he knew more. Should have consulted with Moss again. But damn it, he wanted to do *something*. So he'd taken the risk. Maybe screwed it up. He just didn't know.

Hai ran a hand over his mouth. "We all need to make a coordinated statement. All of the geek stores in town. And it needs to be posted in every shop window. A zero tolerance statement."

Charlie leaned back against the counter. It was his turn to cross his arms over his chest.

"You think that's a bad idea?" Hai asked.

Charlie shook his head. "No. I think it's a good idea, and

goes along with what we were talking about a few days ago. But I'm thinking Sam is right. It doesn't seem like it goes far enough."

"Right?" Sam said. "Like you said, Hai, someone already firebombed us. In light of that, a statement seems a little weak. So what *is* going far enough? What does that look like?"

"At least a coordinated statement is a step," Hai responded. "I think we can strategize from there."

They heard a rumbling from outside, and someone smacked against one of the big plateglass windows out front.

Charlie's head snapped around. There was a small crowd outside the store.

"What the…?" Sam said.

"Sam, lock the doors!" He turned then. "You kids, get in the back!"

"What's happening?" one little white girl asked.

"We don't know, sweetie. But I just want you all as far away from the action as possible. If anything happens, you all can lock yourselves in the bathroom, or go into the stockroom, okay? Zion?"

Zion nodded and stepped toward the group of pre-teens. "Come on back with us, Marla. We'll be fine."

Sam hadn't moved quickly enough. Two shaved-headed white dudes shoved at the door as she fought to keep it closed. Hai joined her, both of them pushing back at the heavy, safety-glass door. Charlie loped toward them, and shoved his shoulder in between his friends. He felt the door slam against fingers and heard a "Fuck!" before releasing it for a second and slamming it shut again.

"Lock it!"

Sam finally got the keys in and the locks *chunked* into place.

More bodies slammed against the windows.

"They better not break those," Charlie said.

"What are they screaming?" Hai asked. His face shone with sweat.

It was hard to make out distinct words in the midst of the roaring and pounding. Charlie stepped away from the door, giving Sam and Hai room to move. They stood two feet from the door, staring out at the roiling crowd. The Hack-Master Nazis were out there, along with skinheads, and what looked like bikers. Most of the people, though? Looked like cleancut, upper-middle-class assholes, salted with hipsters.

Meaty fists rapped against the glass. Someone swung a sign at the large window to the left of the door. It bounced back and hit two other people, who turned on the sign bearer. The sign bore a big red othala rune, a diamond shape with legs; although unlike the one in Charlie's book, this rune had little upturned feet at the bottom. It was the rune of inheritance. Family. Clan.

Every twisted, snarling face outside was pale, some of them edging toward red from the exertion of shouting.

The words came through then, loud and clear, ringing through Charlie's skull.

"White pride. White power," Hai said. "Stupid bastards."

"We're not kicking ass today," Sam replied. "But we're gonna kick their asses someday. I swear it."

A man's blue eyes caught Charlie's through the glass. It was No Socks with the dark-haired man.

"Gloves are fucking off, motherfucker," Charlie said, staring him dead in the eyes. "You're going down."

17
─────

RAQUEL

The café was pretty busy. Raquel and Cassie were both in the groove, making sandwiches, serving up lattes, refilling the water pitchers, wiping tables, and greeting customers. A normal day. Tangible and real. Thank the Goddess.

It sounded as if there was some sort of parade coming down the street. Raquel caught snatches of sound from the distance as the café door opened and closed.

She rolled her shoulders and smiled at the next customer, a Latinx man in work clothes.

"What can I get you today?" He ordered a pot of tea and corn muffin. She put in the drink order and took the glass dome from the pastry stand, breathing in the scent of cornmeal and sugar.

Cornmeal and sugar were some favorites of Yemọja.

Yeah. Raquel needed a day like this. Simple. An uncomplicated day of just being a neighborhood resource and running her business. Making some money. She needed a break from the drama. She wanted her son safe, but she also wished he didn't have to deal with the situations that were threatening him. And as for the ancestors, and Yemoja, and the coven? For now, there seemed to be a truce. She still wasn't feeling like her former witchy, badass self, but she didn't feel completely lost anymore, either.

I think this is all gonna work out okay, she thought.

She wasn't even going to *think* of Charlie. At least, that was what she told herself, which was a total lie. She couldn't *not* think about him. Her body was so wired for him, it was ridiculous. It had been way too long since she'd had sex with someone other than her favorite vibrator.

"That'll be five dollars and fifty cents," she said to the man. Oh, Goddess. Don't think of vibrators and Charlie's broad shoulders and big hands in the same breath. And really don't think of kissing him in front of her house for twenty minutes last night, as if she were a teenager with parents waiting up.

The sounds of people outside increased, resolving themselves into shouting and stomping. Raquel's head shot up from the cash register she quickly counted out the man's change.

"What the hell is that?" Cassie came up beside her. "It doesn't sound good."

"It sounds like it's close," Raquel replied. "Too close."

A few customers were already shoving their way out the front door to see what was up. The open door let in more sound. Definitely shouting. Cassie and Raquel both ran outside

"Shit," Cassie said. "They're outside Owlbear."

Raquel's blood ran cold in her veins and she froze in place, staring down the sidewalk to where, sure enough, a small crowd pushed and swarmed. Just three blocks away.

Fight or flight Raquel? she asked herself. *Fight or flight?*

So much for her simple day.

"It's those damn Nazis Charlie was complaining about," she said.

Her body flashed hot and cold. Hot and cold.

"Oh no." Raquel's fear spiked. "Zion's there."

She started running, apron flapping around her thighs. Thank Goddess she'd put on sneakers that morning instead of restaurant clogs. Cassie would take care of the café. She just needed to get to her son. She ran towards the teeming mass of people shoving each other on the sidewalk.

She heard fists pounding on plate glass. It sounded as if they were trying to break into the shop through the massive windows. That was both good and bad. It meant the doors were locked, at least. As she grew closer, the roaring crowd noise distinguished itself into chanting voices.

"White pride! White power!"

"Fuck."

She put on a burst of speed and crashed into the crowd. Shouldering her way through, she saw that it was mostly men, with a few white women sprinkled through. The men had those weird high-and-tight haircuts with the long sweep of hair on top. There were a couple of shaved heads, too.

She should have felt terrified. One part of her brain knew that, but all she felt in the moment was rage. No fear anymore. Just a pure, white-hot rage.

Yemọja, mama ocean, be with me now.

A wave of power smashed through her. A big white man in a dark green button-down shirt turned and shoved her backwards. She reeled, and then, without thinking, her hips pivoted and her right fist smashed out. She heard the crunch as her fist connected with his nose. A burst of blood and then pain rocked down her hand.

The man bent at the waist, clutching his nose, moaning. Raquel shoved her way past him toward the door. She had to get to her son. Eyes wide, she squinted, desperately trying to see past the glare and the colors from people's clothing that bounced off the glass. Charlie stared down at her. His face went completely white and he reached, scrambling to unlock the door.

"Bitch!" Hands on her shoulders. She was spun around. And then, a punch to the jaw, she was down.

Lights out.

Yemoja...

18

———

CHARLIE

The noise was deafening. Terrifying. Charlie didn't know if he wanted to pee or run. He tried to remember the sense of power he'd felt, tried to call it up. To do what Moss had told him.

"Holy…" It was Raquel, staring up at him. Face so angry, and so beautiful. He fumbled keys out of his pocket, racing to unlock the door to let her in.

"Hai! I'm gonna need your backup! Raquel is trapped out there and we have to let her in, without letting in these assholes."

"I don't know how we're going to do that, but I'll do the best I can, buddy. I got your back."

Charlie felt Hai shoulder up behind him, ready to help block the door.

And then Raquel was spun around by a big white man with blood running down his face, staining his button-down shirt. And he saw the man's fist snap out, cracking Raquel across her cheek. She went down.

"Fuuuck!" Charlie bellowed. "You almost ready, Hai! We've got to get her in here!"

Always return to your feet, Moss had said. *Start there, with your connection to the ground. Everything else flows from there. Then take a big breath, and you'll be set.*

He had to try. There were his feet, in their work boots. The floor underneath. His breath was shallow, constricted, bordering on panic.

Slow it down, Charlie thought.

He willed his stomach muscles to relax, just a little bit. And took in what should have been a deep breath, but was at least a less shallow one. It would have to do. He felt calmer, at least.

"Hang on a second, Hai. This is going to be tricky. We're going to need Sam, too."

He risked a glance toward the back of his shop and saw Zion, brown eyes wide. He looked terrified, but had placed himself in front of the other kids. A little warrior. Well, if Zion could be brave, Charlie could too.

"Sam!"

"What?" Her face was pure fury, like the mask of some D&D demon lord.

"Go lock the kids in the storeroom. I don't trust these assholes to not break in once we open the door. Then we need you here. It'll take all of us to get Raquel in."

Sam nodded, mouth a tight line.

"I want to help my mom!" Zion said.

"You can help your mom by keeping all these kids safe, okay?" Sam said. Zion nodded once and began helping her hustle the kids toward the storage room.

Another slam against the door. Charlie whipped back around. He could barely see Raquel. She was buried in a sea of shifting legs and bodies.

"Sam!"

"Coming!" He heard her sneakers as he fumbled the keys into the lock.

"Get ready! You guys have to haul her in. I'll take care of the Nazis."

He braced himself, and felt Hai and Sam get into position.

The lock clunked. Charlie heaved the door open, making himself as big as possible. He felt that power, whatever it was, blast through him. He stood tall, shoulders broad, feet planted.

He felt Hai and Sam reaching around him. Stretching arms between his legs. The shouting from outside was almost deafening.

"White! Power!"

He felt Sam and Hai drag Raquel through his legs and widened his stance, still blocking the door. He didn't dare look down, away from the crowd. Away from the burly, red-faced man who was practically spitting in his face.

And then words were tumbling from his mouth.

"By the power of Thor!" His voice was loud as thunder. "This place is under protection! I bid you gone!"

Someone shoved him. His hands gripped the edges of the doorway. Gritting his teeth, he held on as bodies battered at him. A shoulder slammed into his chest, and breath whooshed from his lungs.

He felt the energy swirling in and around him and shoved out with his mind, imagining a giant pulse echoing out from his solar plexus, smashing into the men trying to breach the doorway.

Just like D&D, the thought flashed through his mind. He shoved again. The men backed off. He felt Raquel's feet slide past his legs. Heard them thump across the threshold, felt a hand tap at his calf.

"Done," Sam's voice said, next to his ear.

He raised his voice again.

"May Thor smite your ancestors! May Thor make a wreckage of your lives, as you would make a wreckage of ours! Let it be known that this place is a safe haven. And the likes of you shall never be allowed across this threshold."

He stepped back, slammed the door, thrust the keys into the lock and shot the bolt home.

Then he turned and look down at the ground, where Hai and Sam were crouched over Raquel.

Her cheek was already beginning to swell, but nothing could mark her beauty. Her fierceness. Her strength.

"Damn." It hit Charlie like a thunderbolt.

He was in love.

19

RAQUEL

Raquel felt as if someone had taken a sledgehammer to her skull. Along with a dull pounding, a sharp pain in her left cheekbone reminded her of the punch.

Her head snapping backward. A roaring sound. Then blackness. Snatches of images and feelings. Getting dragged on the ground. Then blackness again.

Her mouth flooded with spit.

"Sick…"

"Let's roll her on her side. Someone grab a damp towel? And Hai, can I get your jacket?"

Charlie's voice. Firm hands, gentle on her shoulders.

"We're going to scoot you onto your side, okay, Raquel? You took quite the punch."

She tried to open her eyes, but that just made the pain worse. Her stomach flipped.

"Uhhh…" She swallowed hard, just as Charlie eased her onto her side, shoving something soft underneath her cheek. Then there was warmth. Must be Hai's jacket.

Damp, cool cloth on her throbbing forehead. Her aching cheek.

"Just take some breaths, okay, Raquel? Zion, hold this cloth against her forehead, okay?"

"I want to sit up." Her voice sounded like the croaking of a raven, but at least the cloth on her head was helping some.

"I don't think that's a very good idea." Whose voice was that? Female. Sam.

Raquel lurched up onto her elbows—ouch, that hurt—her stomach flipped again, and she puked up a stream of soup, followed by bile.

"Sorry," she croaked out. But she really didn't want to lie down again.

"Raquel, look at me," Hai said, face peering at her intently. She struggled to focus. "Follow my finger."

She thought she did, but wasn't sure if her eyes tracked correctly. All she knew was that trying made her stomach feel weird again.

The sounds of shouting and pounding continued beyond the glass windows. They had dragged her to the other side of the counter, partially protected.

Though if the Nazis broke through, she was toast.

"Anyone got a flashlight?" Hai again.

"My phone," Sam replied. "Take it. I want to watch the damn doors."

Where was Charlie? Zion was crouched to one side, looking really worried, but she couldn't see Charlie.

Then she felt him. His thighs supported her back. She smelled the warm, sunshiny scent of his skin. The almost-too-strong smell of his laundry detergent. Raquel relaxed back against him. Home.

A teeny-tiny voice in the back of her head tried to tell her that was a dangerous thought. She swatted it away and let his warmth and strength surround her.

"Sorry, Raquel, but I have to check your pupils," Hai

said. He reached a hand toward her face and it was all Raquel could do to sit still and let him touch her. Her cheekbone throbbed and her head pounded so hard it still made her woozy. Hai gently pried her left eyelid apart, shone the ersatz flashlight in her eye, then moved to the other.

"Well, I'm no Bones McCoy, but it doesn't look like you have a concussion. It probably wouldn't hurt to get you checked out by a real doctor, though."

"No. No. Just let me sit here for a while. Can I have that cloth, baby?"

Zion had started twisting the damp washrag into knots in his small, dark hands. He smoothed it out and handed it to Raquel. She wiped it over her face. The wet felt good, though she wished that it was cooler. Her body was cold, but her head was hot.

Weird.

"Can I make you some tea, Momma?"

"That's a good idea, Zion," Charlie said, before she could respond.

Zion must have been looking at Charlie behind Raquel's head, because she saw something change in his face. He went from worried to determined. She wondered what the look they had shared meant. Then her beautiful son rose up and loped off to the little kitchen area she knew sat between the gaming tables and the washrooms.

"He's a good kid." Charlie's voice hummed in his chest, rumbling against her back. "But you scared him half to death. Me too."

"Sorry," she croaked out again. "Had to make sure he was okay."

The gentlest kiss to the side of her forehead. "I don't blame you, but fuck, it was terrifying to look out the door and see you there." He cleared his throat. "And see you go down. Gods, Raquel, I want…"

Zion came back then, holding out a mug of tea. Smelled like peppermint.

"Do you need me to hold it for awhile? It's kind of hot."

"Hot sounds good." She was shivering. Every part of her not in contact with Charlie felt cold. Almost numb. She handed Zion the rag and exchanged it for the blessed mug of tea. The scent of it wreathed her head, easing some of the pounding.

"*White Pride!*"

"Don't those assholes ever shut up?" Raquel asked.

That made Zion grin, at least. A three-second ghost of a smile, before the half-worried, half-angry look settled back across his face. He was too damn young to have that look as often as he did. He especially shouldn't be having it because of his mother.

Zion sat down, cross-legged, next to her, and placed a hand on her leg. She looked down. Her jeans were ripped. Her elbows felt scraped to shit so she bet her sweatshirt was ripped, too. And she still had on her red work apron.

"You're pretty badass, mom."

"Thanks, Zye."

She sipped at the tea. The mint tasted good. Felt good, too, rolling down her throat. She needed Tempest or Moss, though, to work some of their healing energy on her.

"Were you scared?" he asked. His brown eyes were steady, searching her face.

"I was," she replied. "A little. But mostly, I felt pissed off. Were you scared?"

"Yeah. I helped get the other kids into the storeroom. We were locked in, but I could hear Charlie shouting your name. It kinda freaked me. You know? But I was pissed off, too."

"I bet." She leaned forward, out of Charlie's encompassing embrace, toward her son. Her head swam, and she paused a moment. Closed her eyes. Tried to slow her breathing down. The vertigo passed.

"You sure we don't need to get you to the hospital?" Hai asked.

"No. Please. If I'm not well enough to stand in half an hour, Charlie can drive me there."

Then she looked at her son. "Can I get a hug?"

He rocked forward on his knees, and leaned into her. It was worth the pain from the pressure on her chest and arms. Damn. Her ribs felt bruised. She hadn't noticed that before. But then, all she was noticing was the feel of Zion, threading his arms so carefully around her neck. He smelled like boy sweat and licorice.

She started to cry.

"I'm gonna learn how to fight, Mom. I'm gonna learn how to kick those assholes 'til they hurt."

"I know you are, baby. And I'm gonna help you do that."

"So am I," Charlie said.

She just wished, in the Yemoja's name, that they didn't have to.

And she wished her son wasn't still being bullied by the children of the angry mob outside.

20

CHARLIE

What a fucking day.

The crowd of white supremacists had finally cleared out. Between a squad of backup geeks called down by Hai and Sam, and a couple of Portland police cars showing up—likely alerted by neighboring shops. The folks inside Owlbear having been too busy taking care of casualties to call—the HackMaster Nazis and their friends hadn't lasted out an hour.

A few of the men had been taken away; whether they were actually arrested or not, he wasn't sure. Looked like one of them was the guy who'd clocked Raquel, which gave Charlie some satisfaction.

Charlie was glad they were gone, but the way everything had gone down still sat uneasily with him, including half lying to the cops in order to protect Raquel. The last thing she needed was to get hauled in, too. The police seemed skeptical, but took Charlie, Hai, and Raquel's word that she'd just been trying to get to her son.

Which was true. But you never knew how it would all look on paper.

The shop felt too quiet now. They'd managed to call all the children's parents and get them picked up, then closed the shop for the rest of the day. Neither Charlie nor Sam had the bandwidth to deal with concerned neighbors or customers who wandered in for game night, not knowing anything had happened. There were only so many times a person could relive a story in one day.

Alejandro was burning some incense mixture in an abalone shell set on the long checkout counter. Copal and benzoin, he had said. Whatever it was, it smelled good, and was actually making Charlie feel better.

Sam, Moss, Zion, and Alejandro had all stayed behind to help. Brenda had shown up to take Raquel home. Raquel was still refusing to go to the urgent care clinic or the hospital, but had been able to stand up without puking, so Charlie had to be okay with it. He'd promised to bring Zion home later. The boy had really wanted to stay.

Charlie couldn't blame him. The urge to *do* something in situations like this was strong.

Charlie looked at boy, who was helping Moss set out some ritual tools. It was clear the kid knew his way around the weird, witchy stuff, and not just from playing D&D. Charlie wondered what it must have been like, growing up with a witch for a mom, and other witches coming in and out of your house all day long.

Pretty different from his dad's old Army buddies, and their club that Charlie was growing more suspicious of every day. Had his dad really been a died-in-the-wool white supremacist? Not just a garden variety clueless white person, racist by default?

A couple of years ago, Charlie would have said no. But between the little bit he'd been able to go through his dad's stuff, and some of the comments from his buddies—both at the funeral and in emails—and then the comment from fucking No Socks, he was pretty troubled.

Time to face your shit, Charlie. You can't confront these assholes without confronting yourself. He gritted his teeth at the thought, but knew that his conscience was correct. There was no way he was going to let the blatant racists get away with shit, but there was no way he was letting himself off the hook, either. All he had to do was remember some of the "jokes" from his childhood, and he wanted to hang his head in shame.

Hai came up beside him and leaned against the counter. He waved away some of the increasing incense smoke. Speaking of which...

"This isn't going to set off my smoke alarm, is it, Alejandro?" Charlie asked. "I don't want the sprinklers to go off and ruin all the stock."

Alejandro shrugged. "Shouldn't. The ceilings are high enough and the room is huge. That firebomb the other day didn't set off the system, did it?"

Charlie winced, and had to admit the man was right. Fuck. He shrugged at Alejandro. On one hand, he was glad his shop hadn't been wrecked by water damage, but on the other hand, if he hadn't been home? He wondered if the whole building would have gone up. Add that to the list of things to get checked.

"Besides, if we don't get this space cleansed, cleared, and protected, my sister will have my ass, and my nephews won't be setting foot back in the store."

Alejandro went back to setting things up with Zion. Moss was hunched over one of the gaming tables in the back, working out the proper runes.

Hai gestured to the abalone shell.

"So, you're actually going to try to use magic to protect

the place?" he asked. Hai sounded slightly skeptical, but interested, too. Typical geek. Any magical system was going to intrigue him, even if he mostly thought it was all fantasy bullshit.

"That's the plan," Charlie replied.

"It's cool, I guess. But we still have to come up with that bigger plan. We're gonna have to call that meeting we've been talking about. The situation just went from about a Defcon 4 to Defcon 1."

That was the truth.

"Okay. I think I've got it!" Moss said from the back. He shuffled some papers together and loped up to the counter. "Look at these runes, Charlie. You too, Zion, Alejandro. Check them over and make sure they're what we need."

Charlie looked down at the top paper on the small pile and felt punched in the gut. It was all he could do to not bend in half, gasping for breath. It felt as if hands gripped each side of his head, pulling on his hair, pressing on his temples. His whole body began to throb, pulsing with his heartbeat. His skin flushed and sweat popped out on his forehead.

"What the hell is this?" he asked.

"You okay, man?" Alejandro asked.

"Here, sit down," Moss said, guiding Charlie to one of the tall stools behind the counter. "Tell me what's happening."

Charlie sat on the padded stool and leaned on the counter, head cradled in this hands. "I'm not sure. Just looking at that bindrune made me feel like I'd been punched. And now...like I'm on fire or something. It's as if... something is pulling and pushing on me at the same time. Pressure."

He could feel Moss leaning close to him, but couldn't

even open his eyes to look at the witch. "Does it feel similar to when Thor came through you in Raquel's café?"

"Thor came through you?" That was Zion. Just great. Raquel's kid was here and Charlie was a mess. Way to impress.

Charlie heaved in a huge breath and forced himself to sit up and look at Zion. The boy's eyes were huge. "Yeah. At least, I think so."

"That's so dope," Zion said.

"If you say so." Charlie forced a smile out, even though it took everything he had. Then he turned to Moss. "What is that rune?"

"The bindrune combines back to back thurisaz runes— thorns, for the frost giants, but also for your man, Thor." Moss grinned. Charlie wanted to punch him. "There's also elhaz mirrored up and down, see? Extra protection." Moss pointed to the forks facing up and down inside the diamond shape that Charlie figured were the mirrored thorn runes.

"And then that combination forms gebo, that big X. The Gift. I figure Owlbear is a gift to the community, and offering protection to the community keeps the gift moving. Right?"

It made sense to Charlie, in the dim part of his brain that wasn't fighting the pressure that seemed to be building from both inside and outside of him.

"You've got to let go, man," Alejandro said. "You're fighting it. That's why you feel so sick. You have to let whatever's trying to come through you, come through."

"You just let random shit come through *you*, Alejandro?" Charlie spat out.

Alejandro sighed. "No. And I'm not asking you to, either. But if we're calling on the Gods for help, and one of those Gods already marked you?" He shook his head. "Then, yeah,

I'd let that shit come through. It isn't random, and you know it."

It was still strange to see someone dressed like a GQ model or a businessman talk so seriously about magic and the Gods, but Charlie figured if he was in love with a woman like Raquel, he'd better get used to all of this.

What the hell had his life come to?

"Okay. What do I need to do?"

Moss stood up straight. "Alejandro, shop clear?"

Alejandro sniffed the air, and unfocused his eyes, turning clockwise, hands held palms out as if he were sensing something in the air. "Yep. Clear," he said, eyes coming back into focus.

Moss looked at Charlie. "What you need to do is slow your breathing down. Stand up again, as tall as you can. Then call on Thor. Ask him to help us. Meanwhile, Alejandro, Zion, and I are going to cast a protective sphere around this entire building, top to bottom. Then you and I will set the bindrunes. Okay?"

Charlie nodded, then did as he was told. He stood, and did his best to plant his feet solidly on the shop floor. The other two men and the boy took up position, and began making gestures and speaking words. Charlie didn't pay any attention to them, other than to notice they were there, and working. He focused on his breath. Breathing more deeply did take away some of the sick feeling in his gut.

He rolled his shoulders to loosen them up. Flexed his fingers.

Charlie felt the change inside Owlbear as the other three slowly circled the space. He felt it when they arrived at the place they started.

Then he called on Thor. *God of thunder, you of the mighty hammer...* The sense that this was all stupid and he was being made a fool of prickled on the edges of his skin. He took another breath, and dismissed the embarrassed feeling as best he could. He tried to breathe in from the bottom of his stomach muscles, and then let his chest expand as it filled with air. Rocking on his feet, he stood a little taller, then began again.

God of thunder, you of the mighty hammer, lend us your protection. Make this a safe space for those who are willing to obey the contract of hospitality. Help me to protect the children that walk through my doors. Lend me your strength, your certainty. Help me to be of service. Charlie wasn't sure where the words were coming from, but just let them enter his mind and speak through his heart. *And if necessary, help me to smite any asshole that messes with my home, my livelihood, or the people under my protection.*

He was surrounded by a sense of certainty, and filled with a strength and power he would never before have called his own.

Charlie saw Zion lift his arms and gesture toward something above his head, then sweep his arms down to mirror the gesture toward the floor. Charlie could feel that Zion was tracing symbols above the roof of the building and deep beneath the foundation. Again, he'd never felt anything like it before.

But he wanted to feel this way again.

Moss, Alejandro, and Zion all looked his way.

"You call him?" Alejandro asked.

Charlie nodded.

"Then let's activate some runes," Moss said.

Charlie saw the shapes shimmering in front of him. One strong, upright line, supporting a diamond shield and two crossed staves. The bindrune. Elhaz. Thurisaz. Gebo.

Moss pricked Charlie's right ring finger with a small

needle stick, then pricked his own with a fresh stick. He smeared a line of blood down his own forehead, and gestured for Charlie to do the same. Then Moss licked the blood from his fingertip.

So did Charlie.

"We offer our blood for the protection of others, so that no more blood shall be spilled in this space," Moss said. "And we make this offering to feed the runes that will protect us all."

Moss turned to the North, and began to trace the bindrune in the air. Charlie paused for a moment, watching, then called on Thor's power, and traced the symbol in the air.

It felt real. Solid. Tangible.

He turned with Moss, toward the East. Together, they traced the symbol in the air, then pressed it outward, until it sank into the walls themselves.

Charlie felt as if he'd been born to do this magic.

God-touched, he traced runes into the air, as if nothing else in the world mattered.

21

RAQUEL

The whole coven was gathered in Raquel's living room. She was too damn tired and sore to make it all the way to their usual attic ritual space. Zion was in his bedroom, headphones on, watching a video. Charlie had dropped him off an hour before, which was sweet. Alejandro or Moss could have just as easily dropped off her son, but it was clear Charlie had wanted to see her.

She saw it in his eyes. And the way he looked at her mouth. Like he wanted to kiss her, but wouldn't. Not while she was lying on her big red couch, injured. And not in front of her coven and her son. Not yet.

But he'd given her one of those "I'll be seeing you soon" looks before he'd left. And Raquel had wrapped that around her like the cashmere throw Brenda had tucked her up in when she'd brought her home. If she hadn't been so damn worried, tired, angry, and in pain, she would have spent the evening daydreaming about Charlie's broad shoulders and full lips.

But there wasn't time for it. Now was the time for magic. Simple, healing magic first, and once Arrow and

Crescent Coven figured it out, battle magic. Magic that would bring a reckoning to these assholes who had fire-bombed Owlbear, punched her in the face, and sicced their spawn on her son.

Magic that Raquel still needed to learn to trust again, because so far? Magic hadn't been helping the situation much.

Tempest and Tobias were at the head and foot of the red sofa, kneeling on cushions, sending Raquel energy. She felt the healing flow from their hands, twining around her. She also sensed it when Tobias paused and asked energetic permission to enter through the crown of her head. She gave an internal *yes* and felt the power of his fire move into her, warming up the cold places, easing her tension and pain.

Her headache already felt better. The lump on the back of her head must be receding. Her elbows still stung, but not as badly as before.

Tempest raked her hands down through the air just two inches above Raquel's legs. The aches and pains receded with each pass of her fingers.

Raquel groaned.

"Am I hurting you?" Tempest asked.

"No. Feels good."

The other witches talked quietly, ensconced in over-stuffed chairs, cushions, and footstools around the coffee table, in front of the dormant fireplace. A fire would have been nice, but Raquel couldn't see building one just so she could sit in her living room for a couple of hours. The house didn't need heating, despite the on-again, off-again late April rains.

"British witches fought Nazis in the Battle of Britain," Moss was saying.

"And wise women in Kenya fought British Colonials," Lucy countered.

"Biddie Early used magic to burn out landlords in Ireland," Tobias replied. "I did some research on her after we went up against those developers last autumn."

Raquel sank more deeply into the couch cushions and let the healing wash over her. She couldn't summon enough energy or brain power to contribute to the conversation.

"Point is, people have always used magic and sorcery to combat oppression," Lucy continued. "In Ireland, in Mexico...pretty much everywhere you look. So, there's precedent for it."

"There's precedent in Arrow and Crescent," Moss replied. "Diana seems to want us to hunt down evildoers in Portland. Look at how many situations we've been in just in the last year alone."

The Goddess Diana was the matron of the coven, though individuals had relationships with their own Gods and Goddesses as well.

"Yeah." Selene nodded in agreement. "We may as well take on Nazis."

"Get to the root. White supremacy," Raquel finally croaked out.

"Sshhhh," Tempest said.

"Raquel's right about that, though," Alejandro chimed in. "White supremacy is a big problem in Portland, and it contributes to all the other shit we've been fighting."

"No one here is going to disagree on that point," Moss said. "Certainly not this Japanese American witch. But the question is, what are we going to do about these assholes?"

"Well, we seem to have Thor on our side," Alejandro quipped. Raquel could hear that smile in his voice. She smiled, too, and didn't that feel good? If she couldn't have a glass of wine after such a shitty day, at least the healing energy was working well enough that she could smile.

"What do you mean?" Lucy asked. "Who's working with Thor? I would think he'd be a Nazi kind of guy."

"Charlie," Raquel whispered, then cleared her throat and tried again. "Charlie. Thor is coming through him."

Tempest *tsked* at her.

"Oh, *you* hush," Raquel said to the young healer. "You should be glad I'm feeling better."

"And you should be thankful you have two of the best healers in Portland working on you, and relax and accept the healing like they told you. Don't you think you fought enough Nazis today?"

"I think she's okay, Tempest; at least she is from my end. I've given her all she can take right now," Tobias said.

"And I still want to know what the hell is happening with Charlie," Lucy said. "Will someone please explain to me why we think it's okay for some blanquito game store owner to channel a Norse God?"

Tempest gave one last sweep down Raquel's body, then placed her hands on Raquel's feet. Tobias did the same at the other end, cupping Raquel's head in his palms.

"Breathe in," he said.

She did, and felt her whole body relax as she exhaled.

"Thank you," she murmured.

Both healers shook their hands out, then left the room. She knew they'd want to wash their hands. Working on all levels, just the way the coven always taught. Astral, emotional, mental, physical.

Alejandro and Moss tag teamed an explanation for Lucy.

"Also, he was drawn to a book of runes in the shop the day Zion was beaten up. Said he was surprised I carried it, that he thought only Nazis used that system. It was clear that despite his reservations, he was drawn in."

"Yeah, and then Thor showed up in Raquel's café when I was showing him how to make bindrunes. Dude is connected, whether he wants to be or not."

"Thor wants him to be," Raquel croaked out, then took a big swallow of her cooling tea.

She felt her best friend's gaze trained on her. "What?" she asked.

"And who is connected to you?" Brenda asked. The challenge in her voice was clear.

Raquel was too tired to fight back. Too tired to even avoid the question.

"Okay. Yes. Yemọja has been active lately. She wants something, that's for sure. And Ṣàngó…"

"Ṣàngó?" Lucy leaned forward, dark eyes snapping, piece of cheese forgotten in one hand.

Raquel bought more time with another swallow of the soothing tea.

"Zion wanted to train. Martial arts." She gave a little laugh, which sounded harsh even to her own ears. "Turns out the group I found are the Sons of Ṣàngó."

"No shit!" Lucy replied.

"Yes shit." Raquel gave a little smile. "So the Powers seem to be gathering as well."

"Gods and powers. Different magical systems. Different symbol systems. Different energies. All of them being called to the same point and place in time," Brenda said. "I can't say that I feel good about that."

"Yo sé, verdad?" Alejandro said. "It doesn't bode well, does it?"

"But at least they're showing up to help. That's good, right?" Cassiel finally spoke. She'd been quiet, with a deep crease between her ginger eyebrows that wasn't usually there. Now that Raquel thought about it, Cassie must have been scared out of her wits, having watched Raquel run toward that screaming crowd and then have to go in and run the café, not knowing what the hell was going on.

"It's neither good nor bad, I think," Tobias said. He and Tempest were both on floor cushions, leaning up against the red couch.

"The point is," Selene said, twisting a strand of dyed black hair around one of their silver-beringed fingers, "what in Goddess's name are we going to do with all of this? I feel as if too much energy and information are swirling around, everywhere. It feels like we just get clear on one pattern, and another eddy forms two feet away."

Along with being a Tarot-reading master, Selene was the coven's most skilled operative magic worker. They were good at binding and uncrossing magic. The opposite side of the coin from Tobias and Tempest's healing abilities. Hexing and healing, both powers of the witch.

Lucy smacked her palms against her legs. "We need to stop talking in circles and just try something. If Raquel is up to it, why don't we call the Powers and see what they have to say?"

"We'd need Zion for that, too," Alejandro said. "He's the person getting contacted by Ṣàngó."

"No," Raquel said, struggling to sit up.

"Why not?" Selene asked, their voice quiet. Selene knew how to ask a question and not turn it into a challenge.

"Because Zion is thirteen years old and doesn't need to get dragged into this."

Alejandro linked his fingers, as if in prayer, and brought his hands to his face. Thoughtful.

Then he spoke. "Zion is already dragged in, Raquel. Those bullies at school made sure of that, don't you think?"

"Damn it!" she replied. Alejandro was right. "Okay. Go get him. But *ask* him if he wants to do this. It's still his choice."

22

CHARLIE

It was late, and Owlbear was packed with geeks and nerds. Angry geeks and nerds. Every gaming table was full, which was astounding, considering the last-minute call. But it hadn't taken long for word to spread that white supremacists had attacked the shop, twice, and that one of them had punched a Black woman in the face.

Portland had its issues, but when things got bad enough? People rallied in support.

Charlie and Hai stood between the tables and the main wall of the shop, so they could still see the front and the doors, in case anything else went down. Charlie couldn't imagine any Nazis would be stupid enough to make an appearance that night, but you never knew.

Sam leaned against the back wall, close to the mini kitchen and the washrooms. Hoodie up, her mouth was set in a straight line and her arms were crossed over her chest.

The room smelled of model paint, Hai's hair pomade, Rockstar, and coffee.

That feeling of, Charlie guessed he had to call it *Thor*, still buzzed through him. He felt huge. Powerful. Solid in ways he wasn't used to feeling, despite being a big, muscular kind of guy. He wasn't sure if he wanted to fuck or fight or have a beer.

Or all of the above.

This was heady shit, and he hadn't felt this pumped up since high school.

Not since the first time he beat up someone who'd been trying to beat him, for being a comic book and D&D geek. Charlie still felt badly about the beatdown, even while he realized it was the only thing that was going to stop the bullying. After that, the other geeks made sure to hang with him as much as possible. His aura of protection extended far enough that, even though the kids still got pranked, all the worse abuse stopped.

Hai was speaking. "Charlie and I have been thinking of calling a meeting for a while now, to organize against this latest round of creeping fascism in geekdom. We've seen the influx of Nazis in the Furries—foxes with swastika armbands—and the rise of overtly fascistic tabletop games. Plus, just dudes hanging out, intimidating the rest of our clientele...."

He looked at Charlie, who cleared his throat and picked up the thread. "Then Owlbear got firebombed, which was bad enough, and today, as you know, the HackMaster assholes just escalated. They punched Raquel, who owns the café down the street."

"So, what are we gonna do about it?" asked Xena. A tall, busty, broad-shouldered woman with emerald green hair, a purple skull sweater, and combat boots, she owned an online cosplay shop and was a regular fixture in the local scene. "Are you asking us to go kick some ass? Or petition City Hall? Or...?"

The runes around the shop flared to life. Charlie felt a

few people flinch in response, which was interesting, though most of them didn't even notice.

"This is war," he said. "And, just like war, we're going to have to take this step by step. I don't want anyone going into battle unprepared."

Hai and Sam both nodded.

Charlie continued. "We're going to need you strategy geeks to help with this. And we're going to need to figure out a bunch of lines of attack."

Hai spoke up then. "We'll also need an education and propaganda arm. Folks to make memes and fliers."

"And the soldiers?" That was Sam. Leave it to her to get to the point.

"The soldiers are anyone who's willing. But we're going to have to ask for help. And train. Who wants to work on what?"

With a clamor of voices, and a shifting of chairs, around ten of the gathered group spoke all at once.

Charlie raised his hands. "Wait! Sorry about that. What I meant was, figure out what you're best suited to work on. Then why don't we break into working groups and get started? Hai? You take the education and propaganda folks at this front table here. Who wants to head up strategy?"

Two people raised their hands "Okay, James and Tabby. You take the table to the back left. Sam and Xena?"

Both women's heads snapped his way. "You willing to talk to the ground troops?"

"Hell yes," Xena said, as Sam nodded.

"Good. Take the tables in the center of the room."

"Hai and I will float some of the time, and try to brainstorm overall strategy. Anyone who wants to join us, come stand up here and we'll see what space is left once everyone else is settled."

People shoved chairs back, grabbed messenger bags and jackets, and joined their groups.

Charlie's heart was beating strongly in his chest. This all felt right. More than providing a safe haven for geeks and children, this felt like something he'd been born to do.

His father had fought in wars overseas. Charlie would fight this war here, on the ground, in the city he'd been born in.

23

RAQUEL

She could hear Alejandro's voice, and Zion responding, but she couldn't hear what they said.

The rest of Arrow and Crescent got more snacks, tea, and water. Raquel tried to relax, but could already feel Yemoja gathering. She reached for her front pocket, then remembered she wasn't in her ripped-up jeans anymore. Brenda had helped her into yoga pants after she got home.

"Brenda?"

"Yes?"

"Would you do me a favor and look through my jeans pockets? There should be a piece of blue beach glass in the right pocket."

"Sure." Brenda trailed a hand across Raquel's shoulder as she passed the couch, heading for the master bedroom.

Raquel gazed at the painting that hung above the fireplace mantel. A large, fanciful portrait of Zion when he was around age five, it was the image of the Tarot card The Sun. A pang of sorrow stabbed at her heart. Where had that sunny baby boy gone? These bullying bastards had made him into a boy that needed to hide, or punch out at the world. It wasn't fair.

Alejandro came in with Zion, followed by Brenda, who pressed the piece of teal-blue, misshapen glass into Raquel's hand.

"Mom?" Zion rocked back and forth in his stocking feet, hands in the pockets of his jeans. He'd changed into his favorite Ms. Marvel T-shirt. Kamala Khan, the Pakistani Muslim teen from Brooklyn was in her superhero garb, red mask and flowing scarf, yellow lightning bolt, and all. One of her hands was huge, and stretched up to the sky. A strange superpower, but useful, Raquel supposed.

A rush of affection filled her for her powerful little geeky boy. Goddess, she loved her son.

"Hey baby. Did Alejandro explain what we need?"

"Yeah. We need to call Yemọja and Ṣàngó and see what they have to say."

"Sit," she said.

He flopped bonelessly to the floor in the narrow space between the couch and the coffee table, and crossed his legs.

"You okay with this? You've never really done anything like it before."

"I'm a witch, mom. This is one of the things witches do, right?"

Tears pricked her eyes. All she could do was nod.

"Okay. Let's do this thing. Who's going to lead us down? Brenda? Alejandro?"

Her coven mates looked at one another. "We doing this here?" Moss asked.

"No way am I climbing to the attic," Raquel said, "so yes."

"Alejandro, why don't you lead them into trance state?"

Brenda asked. "It's time we started sharing that duty. Get some more people trained."

Alejandro nodded.

"Okay. Circle up, people."

There was a slight shifting of cushions and chairs. Lucy, Moss, and Selene cleared the coffee table into the kitchen, moving back and forth through the swinging door. Tempest and Tobias moved so Zion could sit, back leaning against the couch.

Brenda took a fat beeswax pillar from the mantelpiece and set it in the center of the now-clear coffee table. With a snick of a match and a whiff of sulfur, she coaxed a flame from the wick.

Alejandro stood, and Brenda took his chair. He began pacing in front of the fireplace.

"Slow your breathing down," he said.

Raquel had done this work a hundred times. Her body immediately responded to his words. She felt Zion settle in. They'd practiced just enough for him to be used to opening into a mildly altered state. This would be the most extreme thing she'd ever asked him to do, though. She tried to breathe through her nerves. Her doubts. If her son was facing bullies, he could face one of the ancient powers, right? At least the power was less likely to want him dead.

Unlike these white supremacists. These people who wanted to run the whole damn city. Whole damn country. As if they were entitled to it just because of some quirk of birth and culture.

Fuckers.

Great, Raquel. Start cursing when you're supposed to be opening up to call the òrìṣà of love.

She re-focused her attention on the cadence and sound of Alejandro's words, slowing her breathing again, and dropping her attention into her solar plexus. She relaxed into the embrace of the couch.

Rubbing the piece of sea glass between thumb and forefinger, Raquel slowly broadened her awareness and reached.

Yemoja, she called. *Come to me.*

A gentle wave rolled over her, and the taste of saltwater touched her lips.

Beyond the sound of waves, Raquel heard the beat of the drums.

Ṣàngó.

The parent in her wanted to open her eyes and make certain Zion was okay. The priestess in her kept her eyes shut and broadened her awareness to include him.

She felt her son practically vibrating at the foot of the couch. She felt the drums, powerful, synching with the beating of Zion's heart.

She felt the power of ocean meet the power of blazing fire.

Water and flame. Love and war. The rhythm of waves and the beat of skin on skin, whether that was hand on drum, flesh caressing flesh, or fist against fist, it didn't matter. She felt that in her bones. It was all the rhythm of life itself. Love and war were two sides of the same coin.

:And sometimes we go to war for the things we love.: Yemoja's voice rang inside Raquel's heart.

"We stand tall! We stand strong! We turn the power of fire against them." Zion's voice rang through the living room, drowning out the sound of breathing coveners and the noise of cars going by on the street outside.

"Fire will eat them alive. Fire will destroy them. They seek to tame the powers of thunder and lightning? Thunder and lightning will turn and strike them down!"

A pause, thick and resonant, hung in the air.

"How shall we do this?" That was Alejandro.

Raquel floated in between states, still in the grips of the mighty ocean, hearing the voice of Yemoja, yet able to perceive what was going on in the physical room.

Priestess brain, people called it. The ability to live and move on multiple planes of awareness at once.

The thoughts flickered through her mind like lightning, before the ocean dragged her back down.

:You must always fight from the place of love. It is your greatest strength. Your anger is love. Your rage is love. Your caring is love. Your lust is love. Your sorrow? Is love. Do not give in to despair. Despair and hatred are the enemies of love.:

"You shall face your enemies by meeting them as friends." Zion's voice again, made deeper and more resonant by the power of Ṣàngó. "You shall strike them down only if they refuse to meet you as brothers. You shall meet them on the open field of combat. You shall sing and dance. You shall show them your true power. All the sons and daughters of lightning shall strike down those who seek to use our powers in twisted ways. Untwist the powers, make them true again. Be true within yourselves."

Mother? Raquel asked, not comprehending the words and knowing it was *vital* that she understand.

:What my brother means is, you must each dig deeply and find the core of yourselves. Each shall bring her strength to bear. None shall do the work of any other. You, daughter, shall roll out like a mighty ocean, drowning all who resist you with the power of my love. Others shall dance down lightning. Others shall raise up mountains from the earth.:

And Zion?

Deep laughter rang inside Raquel's head.

:Your son shall lead us all.:

24

CHARLIE

He knew it was a risk, going to a woman's house uninvited, but he also couldn't wait to see her. To make sure she was okay.

Watching Raquel take that punch and go down had terrified him. His stomach leapt to his throat for thirty seconds before the rage took over, filling his head with white noise and blacking out his vision until he wrestled himself into some semblance of control.

If getting Raquel safely inside the shop hadn't been the most important thing, Charlie knew he would have been out in the crowd, swinging a replica broadsword like a big idiot.

He would be in jail tonight if that had happened.

Charlie walked over to Raquel's house from Owlbear after the meeting shut down. The neighborhood was quiet once he turned off the main drag and on to one of the residential streets that would dogleg him to Raquel's. He hadn't realized how close she lived until he'd dropped Zion off that afternoon.

He caught a whiff of night-blooming jasmine and

inhaled deeply, trying to calm his jitters. The meeting with the rest of the geeks had been good, really good, and he was still pumped up from it. The streetlights in this neighborhood were dim and set far apart, the only other lights coming from some of the Craftsman porches, and the courtyard lights in the small apartment building on the corner.

He turned onto Raquel's street, passing three old pyramid-roofed worker's cottages, heading toward the larger Craftsman across the street. He loped over after looking both ways. No cars coming. Everyone was already at home, or working night shift at the bus yard or the bottling factory across the freeway.

"Hey man!" Alejandro was coming down the walk that wound between a large elm and a smaller tulip tree. "What are you doing here?"

The men smacked their palms together, then shook. "Coming to see if Raquel was still up. I couldn't go to sleep tonight without checking on her, but I just got out of a meeting."

"The coven did, too. You're in luck. Brenda's the only one left, and Zion just went to bed."

"How is he?"

Alejandro screwed up his mouth and shrugged. "He'll be all right, I think. It's been a hell of a week."

That was the truth.

"Well, I've got to get home. I've got an East Coast conference call first thing tomorrow."

"Hey, Alejandro?"

"Yeah?"

"Thanks for everything, man."

"No worries, hermano. We've got you."

Charlie stepped aside and let the tall man by, then took a breath and continued up the walkway between the trees.

He raised his fist and knocked on the heavy wood door.

Brenda opened, her dark wavy hair piled high on her head. Silver jewelry winked in the porch light.

"Charlie."

"Is Raquel up for a quick visit?"

Brenda smiled. "She's still ensconced on the couch and we were just trying to figure out if it was worth getting her into bed. I'm sure she wouldn't mind if you came in for a minute."

Charlie nodded and stepped into the foyer.

"Brenda? Who is it?" Raquel's voice hit him just as he turned the corner, taking in the big, bright, sun-filled painting of what looked like a younger Zion above the fireplace mantle. He looked for Raquel, finally catching sight of her face and dreads spread over one end of a big red couch.

"It's me. Sorry I didn't call, but..." He looked around the room, getting a vague impression of comfortable chairs, bright artwork. Wood casings on the doors. Looking anywhere but at her. The woman he loved. The woman whose fragile, creaky-sounding voice filled him with rage all over again. He really wanted to punch out whoever had made her sound so weak.

Raquel was anything but.

"Hey," she said. "It's okay. Thanks for coming to check on me."

"I'm going to take off, if that's okay. Caroline is waiting up for me," Brenda said.

"Don't let me keep you from your hot girlfriend," Raquel croaked out. "Thanks for staying. And for...everything."

And then they were alone. Charlie could hear his heart beating in his chest. He forced his feet to move to one of the chairs grouped around the big red couch and sat.

Leaning forward, he searched her face. The bruise was

purple and green against her dark skin. Her left eye was bloodshot.

"Damn it. How much pain are you in?"

"Enough. Tobias and Tempest helped a lot though, so it's less than it was." She gestured with a squat, heavy glass, half an inch of oily amber swirling in its base. "Brenda gave me the choice between painkillers and bourbon. I chose the bourbon. Want some? Glasses in the kitchen; bottle, as you see, is still here."

Bourbon sounded about right. He fetched a glass from her bright kitchen, and poured himself one finger. Holding it to his nose, he sniffed the potent combination of caramel, tobacco, and cedar.

Taking a sip, he enjoyed the mellow, smooth roll of it across his tongue, and finally sat back in the comfortable barrel chair. Surprising, for a chair picked by a woman, it actually fit his frame.

"So." He cleared his throat. "Alejandro, Zion, and Moss helped me set up protective runes around the shop. Hopefully they'll work better than the sorry-ass ones I tried to put up."

"Most things take time to learn. Why should magic be any different?"

Huh. He didn't really have anything to say in response to that, so he changed the subject.

"The meeting with the geeks went really well, I think. We've got some subcommittees forming to work on different actions. The group was large for the last minute, too. Word spread that you'd gone down and that brought everyone out."

"Huh. I wouldn't expect anyone to know who I was."

Charlie shrugged. "For some people, I think it was hearing that a Black woman had been punched by Nazis in front of a gaming shop was all it took. The fact that you're a parent of a gamer sealed the deal."

"Bastards," she said, taking another sip.

"Bastards," he agreed. "How was your coven meeting?"

"Good. Not a meeting we wanted to be having—we're supposed to be planning Beltane right now—but it looks like the Gods want us to make a move on these assholes." She stared at him then, with one bloodshot and one clear eye. Even battered, she was beautiful. "We're going to have to do some larger coordination. You know that, right?"

"Haven't thought about it yet, but I think you're right."

They sat in silence, sipping their bourbon, neither of them wanting to rehash their meetings or the events of the day.

Finally, Charlie spoke again. "So, what's Beltane?"

Raquel gave a little smile, and snuggled more deeply under her blanket. That caused a wince of pain. "Beltane is my favorite time of year. It's the time when spring is in full force, and you can almost taste summer coming. Here in Portland, everything is growing. Leaves are back on the trees. Birds are building nests. Flowers are spreading pollen everywhere."

"I don't like that last part."

Raquel laughed. "I take your point, but you can't blame them for wanting to have sex, can you? That's really what Beltane is all about. Life moving through everything. Opening up the world. And for most creatures—including most humans—that's all about sex."

"Like, sex, sex?"

"Like, sex, sex. You sound like my son. But it's not just 'sex, sex.' Like I said, it's all about life force. The joy of being alive. Of surviving winter. Of surviving at all."

"But it's about sex, sex too?" Charlie arched an eyebrow.

Damn. The little bit of bourbon, or the release of tension, or something...must be getting to him. Or it was just Raquel. He set his glass down on the coffee table and, with a long lean toward her, was off the couch and crouching at her side.

"Why don't you tell me about that part."

"Well, sometimes when two people really like each other...?"

"Yes?" He leaned in closer. He could feel her breath on his cheeks. Smell her hair oil, and the coffee scent that followed her wherever she went.

"Sometimes they..."

"Raquel? May I kiss you?"

"Yes."

Gently, so gently, he pressed his lips to hers, hands not touching her, because he wasn't sure what was hurt and what wasn't.

She increased the pressure, and flicked out her tongue.

He moaned, and kissed her back, tasting the bourbon on her tongue, before breaking softly away.

"You're so beautiful, Raquel. Seeing you go down today, I..."

He wanted to tell her he loved her, but it was too much, too soon.

"I was so afraid," he finished.

"So was I," she said. "But mostly? I was angry."

"Me, too."

"Kiss me again," she said. "Then I'm afraid I've actually got to try and sleep. I'm exhausted."

"Of course," he said, and lowered his lips to hers.

25

RAQUEL

Raquel drove to the park to pick up Zion from his martial arts class. She would have walked, but figured they could hit the grocery store afterwards, lay in some supplies. Maybe get a treat for dinner. Besides, walking the ten blocks to the park would have likely wiped her out. Her whole body still hurt, and she didn't trust she'd be able to make it there and back again.

The day off work had done her good, she had to admit. She'd soaked in an epsom-salt-filled tub, read a book on òrìṣà practice written by a mambo and academic in New York City—Marta Moreno Vega—and eaten soup for lunch. She should have gotten caught up on laundry, but was too tired.

She'd actually shown up at the café that morning, thinking she should work, only to find that Cassiel had already called Laurel in to take her shift. The former owner, Kelsey, had even said she'd come back in for the rest of the week if Raquel needed, which was incredibly generous.

"What, you think you're the boss now?" Raquel had groused.

Cassiel had stood her ground, skinny arms crossed over her chest. "No offense, Raquel, but your face might scare the customers today. And besides, you're walking like you're a not-so-spry eighty-five-year-old."

Raquel couldn't argue with either of those things. Her ribs ached, and her right elbow throbbed from where it had hit the concrete. The headache had subsided, but still skated around the edges of her temples. Besides, if Raquel was being honest, she wasn't sure she could handle dealing with people's concern. All that emotion coming at her was exhausting when she was already bone tired.

She turned a corner, navigating her little electric Fiat toward the towering pines of the park, slipping the beetle green-car into a parking spot just across the street. Its size was a major selling point. There was practically nowhere she couldn't park. Not that she drove much, both her work and Zion's school being within walking distance of her home.

The scent of the pines soothed her. She paused for a moment before checking traffic and hobbling across the street. There were a lot of people out. Despite the gray day, it wasn't raining, and the air had warmed up to a practically balmy sixty-five degrees. Children shrieked and shouted from the playground. Raquel smiled and took one of the paths that wound around the towering trees, past the picnic tables.

The Sons of Ṣàngó practiced just on the other side of the baseball diamond, so she headed past the playground toward the expanse of grass. A jogger huffed past as Raquel scanned the spaces between the trees, swing sets, and a small group of pre-teens playing tag on the baseball field.

There they were. Red and white shirts, black pants. Bodies moving with grace and power. Raquel could almost hear Ṣàngó's drums beneath all the other sounds of the park. Her hips swayed a little in response. The Powers worked in strange ways. Even in the middle of a city park, they changed the very air.

As she grew closer, her brow furrowed. There was Shawn in his red shirt, coil of dreadlocks tucked up under a black knitted cap. She didn't see her son. Maybe he'd ducked into the rec center on the corner to use the toilet?

Three sets of men and women sparred together, with Shawn and Seye watching closely, occasionally stopping a pair to make some minor corrections to their form. Raquel stepped closer and waved. Shawn looked up, eyes bright over his high cheekbones. He said something to Seye. The mountain of a man nodded in response. Then Shawn walked toward her, filled with coiled energy, looking like some wild, powerful animal.

The thought barely flickered through her, before it was replaced with worry once again.

"Where's Zion today? I thought he was coming after school," Shawn said when he was within conversation distance. "And what happened to your face?"

Her mouth dried up and a shiver ran across the skin on her forearms. She tugged the black sleeves of her sweater down.

"What? He never showed up?"

She swayed on her feet. Shawn held out a hand to steady her. "Let's sit for a minute. You can tell me what's going on."

He led her to a bench next to the path that skirted the edge of the grassy sparring area. She sank down, wiping her hands on her jeans. Despite the chill, she was sweating. What in Goddess's name was going on?

"First of all, what's up with the bruises? And you're walking like you're hurt."

"I was attacked by a group of white supremacists yesterday afternoon. Outside the game store."

She looked at him. His dark eyes were steady on her face, though now they burned with the banked heat of coals ready to burst into flame. Heat rose from his skin, smelling of copal and other, darker resins. His jaw tightened.

"Do the Sons of Ṣàngó need to get involved?"

She paused for one second, then the rush of fear took over again. "I...probably. I can't think about that right now. Right now all I can think about is where the fuck is my son?"

Raquel's chest was tight. She could barely breath. Panic shook her belly. She wanted to leap up and punch something. Anything.

"Slow down a moment. Breathe." Shawn's voice remained calm. Steady. Raquel knew the trick of it, because as a priestess and witch, she had it, too. She didn't care. Didn't want to be soothed and smoothed.

But she forced air more deeply into her lungs anyway, because she knew the man was right.

"What is going on? I don't understand. How has everything *gone so wrong*?"

"We don't know that anything has happened to Zion. Maybe he got caught up in something after school."

She stood then, and started walking through the park, back toward her car.

"Where are you going?"

"To *find* my *son*."

She heard his sneakers on the walkway. Then he was at her side, pacing her, which, given that her right hip ached and slowed her down, and his legs were long, wasn't hard.

"Raquel. We need to be strategic about this. Call his school. And where else? Where else would he have gone?"

She stopped, throat closed, tears of frustration threatening to break free. Damn it.

Yemọja, you have to help me now.

"Owlbear. The game store. He goes there with his friends. But he *told* me he was coming here. After yesterday, he couldn't wait to get back to train."

Shawn shrugged. "Maybe he needed something different. The boy is having a hard time, and it couldn't have been easy for him to see you this way."

No. It couldn't have been. It must have scared him half to death. More than he even admitted yesterday.

Tugging her phone from her jeans, she dialed Charlie.

"Is Zion there?"

She closed her eyes. Dammit.

"No," she said. "I'm here. In the park. He was supposed to come to the martial arts class. He never showed up."

She tried to slow her breathing down again, fighting off the blind panic that threatened to engulf her. Charlie was saying something, but she couldn't make out what it was. Someone wrapped an arm around her, propping her up.

Words. More words. Spots dancing at the edges of her eyes. The trees. Pine. Copal.

"Raquel! Breathe! Breathe! Okay. Down on the ground, sister. Head down. Come on. Easy. Easy. Let's go."

Grass. She was on the grass. Her hand dropped the phone. Panicked voice squawking through the tiny speaker.

"That's right, sister. Slower. Deep breaths."

More people. Feet. Voices. Black pants. Red and white shirts. The Sons and Daughters of Ṣàngó, surrounding her.

Mama. Help me. A soothing wave of ocean. A woman held out a water bottle.

"Drink," she said.

Raquel drank. Water ran down her chin. She coughed.

Shawn's hand on her back, warm between her shoulder blades. Steady.

"Charlie is coming to get you because you are in no condition to drive. You're going to call the school right now, okay? And if Zion isn't there? We're all going to go find your son."

26

CHARLIE

"So where should we start looking?"

Raquel was huddled against the car door, staring out the window. Charlie wasn't sure whether or not she actually saw the trees and the cars going by.

"I don't know," she replied. "I can't imagine where he would be. He's *always* where he said he would be."

Charlie swore under his breath and turned the car in the direction of Zion's school. He'd talked with that guy, Shawn, who said his people would comb the neighborhood on foot.

"Well, we may as well start at the school, since that's the last place we know he was. Or at least we can assume he made it to school today, right?"

Charlie glanced over at Raquel again. That bruise on her cheekbone filled him with fury. Every time he saw it, he replayed the image of her falling to the ground. And added to that image now was the image of her surrounded by people in red, white, and black, on that bench in the park, hunched over herself, looking completely defeated. She was not a woman who should ever look defeated.

Panicked, barreling through that park, past joggers and

Frisbee players, dodging strollers and kids on roller skates, he had run toward the people dressed in red, white, and black.

He couldn't see Raquel.

He needed to see Raquel.

And then there she was, on that park bench, in the center of the small crowd of warriors. A tall, muscular man with some sort of big knit hat had sat next to her, a hand on her shoulder.

Charlie had felt jealous. He still did, a little, even though he knew that was ridiculous. *Don't be an ass*, he thought.

"Raquel? You think he went to school?"

She snapped her head towards him, eyes fierce and filled with pain. "I don't *know*. I just..."

Charlie reached across the car gave her arm a quick squeeze. "All right. It's okay. We'll find him."

Zion's school was only a five-minute drive from the park, but with all the people getting off work and school, it felt as though it was taking forever. Charlie bit back a curse and barreled through stop signs the way he had barreled through the park, looking for Raquel.

When he thought about it for a minute, he was glad that warrior dude, what was his name? Shawn. He was glad Shawn and his people had been with her. The jealousy was stupid. Charlie was just glad Raquel hadn't been alone.

Finally, the school came into view. It was low-slung, yellow-bricked, two-storied, with a long mosaic mural on one side. Turning, they passed the playground. Couple of kids playing hoops on the blacktop. It didn't look as if there were any after-school activities happening outside. Charlie didn't know if that was usual or not.

"I don't see him," Charlie said. Raquel's right hand

gripped the handhold above her door. Her brow furrowed as she searched the grounds.

He turned another corner, and there, huddled on the front steps of the school, was Zion.

"Stop the car!" Raquel unsnapped her seatbelt and reached for the door.

"Raquel, just wait a minute. Let me pull over."

She flung the door open when the car was still rolling. Charlie cursed and slammed on the brakes. Raquel flew out of the car, sneakers smacking as she ran toward the steps. Her gait was uneven. Charlie knew she was still in pain.

Forget about parking. Charlie flung himself out of the car, toward Raquel hunched around her son.

Then he saw the kid's face.

"Motherfucker," he swore softly.

Charlie always thought of himself as a pretty good-natured, easy-going guy. But these days? Didn't take much to fill him with rage. Blinding, white-hot rage. Seeing Zion's busted lip and battered face—seeing the way he held his arms over his ribs, as if breathing hurt—made Charlie want to kill somebody.

What was it about this family? He never much thought about being a father before. But now, it seemed, all his parental instincts had rushed in.

Tears rolled down Raquel's face, but she was steady as a rock, holding on to her son. She held him gently, though, Charlie could see that. Both mother and son were really injured. Charlie crouched down on the steps in front of them.

"Hey Zion," he said softly. "How badly are you hurt?"

Zion shrugged and looked away, swiping a hand across his face, then wincing.

"I'm just trying to figure out if you need to go to the

hospital, kiddo. What do you think, Raquel?" She nodded briefly. Then finally looked at him with one bloodshot and one beautifully clear, brown eye.

"Let's just get to urgent care, see what they say," she said. "My insurance will cover that."

Charlie stood up, "Okay. Zion? Do you need help standing?"

Charlie reached out his arms, giving Zion space to choose. The boy grasped one of his hands, and Raquel took the other. Together, they both helped him stand, as gently as possible. The boy hissed in pain and hunched over his ribs again.

That blinding white-hot sensation flashed through Charlie again.

"Who did this to you?" he asked, in a voice not quite his own.

"Their fathers..." Zion began. "I mean, the fathers. The boys..." Then he looked at his mother, and back to Charlie. "The men..." Charlie could tell the boy was really having trouble breathing.

What the hell was he talking about?

"That's okay, Zion, we can talk about it later. Let's get you to urgent care," Charlie said.

And then? Someone was going to pay.

27

RAQUEL

The smells and sounds of the café surrounded Raquel. The low murmur of conversations, the hiss and sputter of milk frothing, the scents of freshly ground coffee and grilled sandwiches. It helped her relax somehow, despite all the work that always needed to be done, and the fact that she wasn't actually working today.

No matter what, so far her café felt like home.

So did Brenda, sitting at the table across from her, a grilled sandwich and cup of green tea in front of her. Raquel had a sandwich, cup of soup, and coffee. All she wanted was the coffee, but Cassiel and Kelsey had both insisted she take some food.

Brenda was in her usual flowing top, a blue-and-peach number today. The moonstone rested just beneath her collarbone and her wavy dark hair was down, just falling to her shoulders, framing her creamy, narrow face. The face of Raquel's sister in the Craft. Her best friend.

When Brenda had arrived, she'd hugged Raquel gently. It was all Raquel could do to not burst into tears. She felt like shit, and should have met her friend at home, but didn't want Zion to overhear the conversation. He was worried enough as it was. Raquel didn't need to burden her son with more.

So Raquel had asked Brenda to meet up for lunch. She had offered to head up to Hawthorne, but Brenda said she didn't want Raquel to be farther away from Zion than necessary. The thing Brenda didn't voice was that she also didn't want Raquel driving anywhere.

That pissed her off, just a little, but she knew her friend was right. She wasn't thinking straight, and shouldn't be piloting even a tiny vehicle like the Fiat. She'd be the one hurt, and then where would Zion be?

Raquel had really needed to see Brenda, who felt like the only anchor she had left. Not only as co-head of Arrow and Crescent Coven, but as a friend who knew more about Raquel than just about anyone.

Brenda speared her with one of those all-knowing looks she got sometimes, but Raquel ignored it. Brenda just sighed and picked up her sandwich.

Raquel sipped at her coffee, buying time. The frothy coffee drink was contained by one of the big red ceramic cups Raquel loved so much. Today she barely noticed them. Barely tasted the coffee. She did appreciate the warmth, though. Despite the relative late April warmth outside, Raquel had caught a chill she couldn't shake.

She felt so at sea, and not in a good way. All her anchors had been yanked up from the ocean floor. She was drifting with no rudder, and no way to steer. She couldn't even see the stars.

Raquel had never felt so alone. Yesterday had felt like forever, and it'd been a long few days overall.

"They hurt him real bad," Raquel finally said, setting her cup down.

"I'm so sorry, Raquel. How is he today?" Brenda asked.

Raquel ran a hand across her face, carefully avoiding the bruise on her cheek. She felt so damn tired. "Two cracked ribs, so he's just laid up in bed. Nothing to do but wait that out, the doctor said. Bruised up. Sore. Angry. I think his pride is hurt, too."

"They cracked his ribs? Oh my Goddess! What are you going to do?"

"I have no earthly idea. I want to call on every vengeful Goddess and strike them down, that's for sure. I want to call Selene and ask them to whip up the worst piece of operative magic they can think of. I *want* to obliterate them all from the face of this earth. I want to drown them in the sea."

She picked up her latte again, and swallowed some of the milky caffeine. "And I know that none of that is the *right* answer. But I don't know what the right answer *is*. I don't even know if I believe in magic anymore. What good has it done so far? *Nothing.* So I called you."

Brenda squeezed Raquel's hand, then picked up her grilled veggie panini again and took a delicate bite, silver rings flashing. She knew Raquel well enough to keep giving her space. The moonstone at her breastbone drew Raquel in for a moment. She fell into the cold whiteness of it, swimming through it the way she swam on the astral plane. Was the answer there? Was her subconscious trying to tell her...? What? Damn. She had just zoned out in the middle of the café during lunch. Snapping her attention back to physical reality, she took a shuddering breath. Then picked up the big red cup and drank some more of her latte.

"You need to eat," Brenda said.

Raquel looked down at her own sandwich. Her stomach clenched. The thought of eating made her feel ill.

"I don't want to."

"Raquel." Brenda leaned across the small two top table and lowered her voice. "I just watched you leave your body. You are really ungrounded right now and it isn't safe. We need you here. *Zion* needs you here. Look, I don't blame you, but you can't fight this if you keep checking out."

Raquel looked down at her food again, then shoved the sandwich to the side and pulled the cup of chickpea soup into its place. Took a tentative spoonful. Okay. That was okay. She could eat some soup.

"What exactly happened to Zion, Raquel? Are you going to tell me?"

Raquel set her spoon down with a clatter and sat back in her chair. Her breath had stopped in her chest again. Dammit. Goddess send a wave to drown them all. Forcing herself to breathe again, she struggled to drop back into her center.

"The kids of those men? The ones the cops took in for questioning, all too briefly?" She spat the words from her tight throat. "They found Zion when he was walking from school to the park and beat the shit out of him. Told him..."

Her fists clenched. She took another breath.

"Told him to 'tell his black bitch of a mother that there was more where that came from.' For both of us."

"Damn them. You going to file a police report?" Brenda asked.

Raquel shrugged. "I don't know. A Black woman's word against a bunch of white dudes? Doesn't usually go so well. And as fast as they let those assholes go? I don't trust that some of them aren't on payroll, you know?"

"Okay. So what can Arrow and Crescent do?"

"I don't know. That's part of the trouble. Yemoja was clear that I need to fight this from a place of love. But right now? I can't access that *at all*. I'm so filled with rage and fury that it's all I can do to keep from screaming and running through the streets with a sword. Love? She wants me to fight from a place of *love?*"

Her vocal cords were so tight they were about to snap, from the effort of keeping her voice low. Maybe meeting in the café had been a mistake.

Brenda's eyes filled with tears. Raquel could feel her friend's heart, opening, reaching to enfold her. She couldn't take it. She couldn't fall into the soft strength of Brenda's embrace. Not now. She'd lose it all. Forever.

"I want to kill them," Raquel whispered. "And I can't figure out why that's even wrong."

"We're going to figure this out, sister of mine. Arrow and Crescent, and whoever Charlie is organizing…and from the sounds of it, the Sons of Ṣàngó, too. We're going to do what it takes." There was steel in Brenda's voice. For all that she was a priestess of air, she was still one of the strongest people Raquel knew.

Raquel nodded, unable to speak. But just as she had in the park the day before, she heard drums.

They sounded like the drums of war.

28

___

CHARLIE

Laurelhurst was one of the prettiest manicured parks in Portland. Charlie loved the wild parks across the river, of course, and hiked the volcanoes that ringed the city, but Laurelhurst was pretty much perfect for picnicking families, joggers, badminton and basketball players, and neo-hippie slackliners.

Charlie inhaled the scent of grass and the Christmas-tree smells of the towering Douglas firs, which were the oldest trees in the park. They were joined by dawn redwoods and the spiced-sugar scent of katsura.

The sun filtered through the trees, warming the path that wound through the gentle slopes of the park down to the duck pond. Raquel said the coven would be setting up the Maypole toward the western side of the twenty-seven-acre park.

Beltane. Charlie had never thought of it until a week ago, and here he was, off to a ritual. Oh, sure, he'd seen Maypoles and all that, but had just never much thought of the significance. It had been way too many years since that half-drunk pizza-and-beer geek night when they watched *The Wicker Man.*

That seemed like a long time ago, all things considered. Now here he was possessed by Gods—though his internal jury was still out on what exactly that meant, but something sure as hell was going on—channeling ancient runes, and heading to a ritual in the park with a bunch of witches. Charlie grinned and shook his head. He really had stepped straight into an RPG.

The grin didn't last long, though. He wasn't at the park for the fun, sexy-times ritual Raquel had described. Alejandro and Moss had asked him to come as backup. They didn't trust the city right now, and who could blame them? So he wasn't really here for the ritual, he was here for muscle, along with the men and women who trained with the Sons of Ṣàngó. He'd asked if they needed him to call in some of the geeks, too, but Alejandro had shaken his head.

"We don't want to call in all of our resources in case we need them later," Alejandro had said.

And didn't that just make Charlie feel uneasy. The thought that "later" was all too damn likely. Damn these Nazi assholes, anyway. Charlie hated the way they were making everyone run around, scared and angry. He hated beyond hate that they had harmed Raquel and Zion. He wondered if the boy was even well enough to attend the celebration today.

And he hated that it looked as though Raquel's coven was preparing for some longer, drawn-out war. This wasn't just a blip on the radar. This was a whole phalanx of submarines, lurking underneath dark water.

Anyway, that was a lot of hate to be carrying on such a gorgeous day. He tried to relax and enjoy the late morning. Children shrieked after the ducks in the big pond. A flock of

Canada geese ate calmly on one of the open slopes, under the sun. People scraped down the communal barbecue grills in the picnic area.

And there was the coven.

There was Raquel.

She looked better today. Her hair was down, coiling over her shoulders. She wore a bright teal T-shirt over slim jeans that hugged her curvy hips. A crown of white, orange, and purple flowers rested on her brow. Despite the fading bruise, Raquel looked beautiful. His heart skipped in his chest and sweat broke out on his forehead.

Yep. It was love.

"Hey man!" Moss greeted him. The small man wore an *Earth First* T-shirt in faded purple. He also had on a crown, this one of leaves and greenery. He was speaking with a dapper white man in a yellow-striped vest and a black top hat festooned with flowers.

"Charlie, meet Joshua, Joshua, meet Charlie."

The men shook hands and smiled.

"Pleased to meet you, Joshua. Moss, I assume I'll get a debriefing on what you all need from me in a bit? I need to say hello to Raquel."

"Yeah. As soon as the Sons of Ṣàngó get here, we'll confer."

He slid past a small group of older, white-haired women wearing Wyrd Sisters T-shirts over long, flowing skirts. They really looked like witches to him, unlike the Arrow and Crescent crew, who were all on the younger side. Brenda and Alejandro, both fortyish, seemed like the oldest of the bunch.

Raquel waited for him, a slight smile playing on her lips. She gestured to the blanket at her feet, which Charlie finally saw was strewn with flowers, greenery, and spools of copper wire.

"Time to make your crown," she said.

"No way you're getting me in one of those," he replied.

"Chicken?"

"How am I supposed to look tough and scare off assholes with a wreath of roses strapped to my head?"

"That's your problem," she said. "If you aren't tough enough to pull it off, I'm not sure we should have invited you."

He leaned in for what he planned to be a quick kiss of greeting. Hands on his arms, she pulled him closer, deepening the kiss. By the time she pulled away, he would have worn flowers wherever she wanted them.

Charlie cleared his throat. "No Zion?"

Her face shuttered slightly, dimming the light in her eyes. "No. He's still in a lot of pain, and I didn't want him getting jostled. Not with those ribs. He was upset about it. He's been to every Beltane since he was born. But he was also too out of it to argue much. I almost stayed at home, but he insisted I had to come, to carry both of our wishes around the pole."

"Who's staying with him?"

"My mother," she replied.

Charlie heard his name called, and whipped his head around. Moss and Alejandro waved him over. The Sons and Daughters of Ṣàngó had arrived.

"I've got to go meet up." He kissed her again.

The next hour flew by. He met with the Sons of Ṣàngó and a few other people the coven trusted to do backup, including the dandy, Joshua, whom Charlie had met when he first arrived. A neat hole was dug in the center of the grassy field, and the Maypole was raised, with a bright rainbow of ribbons neatly paper clipped into coils, waiting to be unfurled.

Charlie could see how this would be a beautiful ritual, smack in the midst of spring.

But he also couldn't mistake the fact that he and a bunch of people were present, not to enjoy a celebration, but to protect it.

Just in case.

Along with the Sons of Ṣàngó crew and the other people deputized to stand guard, Charlie found his way on the edges of the welcoming circle that Brenda cast around the space, using what looked like a willow wand. She had explained that this circle was simply a way to mark off the space for dancing, but that people could come and go as they wished. It was a pretty ritual. After Brenda had traced the sphere, red-haired Cassiel had recited a poem to the directions. Then Selene stepped up and addressed the gathering.

"Today is Beltane! The time between the equinox and solstice. It is a day some of our ancestors honored the powers of renewal. We do that today, dancing the Maypole, invoking the powers of beauty, love, and community into every heart." Selene laughed then. "And those of you who want to? Feel free to invoke the power of sex!"

The crowd whooped and hollered at that. The ribbons shimmered in the air.

The drums started an opening beat, the dancers grabbed the bright ribbons, unspooling them, some dancers facing clockwise, and some counterclockwise. And then the dance began.

Raquel had two ribbons in her left hand instead of one. One for her, one for Zion. The dancers stepped in and wove their ribbons under, then stepped outward and wove the ribbons over the strand.

Charlie stood on the edges of the circle, grinning ridiculously, clapping in time with the drums.

Ready. Just in case.

Other people passing by paused to watch. Others joined right in. Children ran in a shrieking circle around the pole, and a couple of young Goths in black cargo pants and lipstick left their picnic and were happily weaving ribbons for a turn or two. People stepped in and out, trading off time on the ribbons. It seemed that everyone was weaving wishes. Charlie regretted not being able to do that, too.

Selene paused next to him, dressed in black combat boots and a flowing black shirt patterned with richly colored flowers. They also wore a flower crown.

"See how people are trading off?" they asked him. "That's part of how the ritual works. Just like joy, magic shared is magic doubled. Every person's wish helps bolster the wishes yet to come."

Selene looked at Charlie, one sharp black eyebrow quirked.

"What do you wish?" they asked.

"I'm not going to tell you that!" he bantered. "Doesn't that diminish the power, or something?"

Selene shrugged. "It depends on the magic and the intention. But you keep your secrets, Charlie. Though I bet half the people here can guess. At any rate, if you'd like, I'm happy to carry your wish into the weave."

Charlie paused. Did he want that? Did he want to weave his wishes in with these people?

He shook his head. "No thanks. Maybe next year."

"Fair enough." With a smile, Selene walked off in their stompy boots to rejoin the dance.

The day really couldn't have been more beautiful. The sun was out. The park was filled with laughter, and the scent of trees and smoking barbecue grills. And there was a gorgeous, multicolored basket weave building itself around the pole.

"What the fuck?"

The words cut through the sounds of drums and laughter and then Charlie and the Sons of Ṣàngó were surrounded by a moving scrum of those damn high and tight, floppy-topped haircuts. Moss, Alejandro, and Lucy all joined in, trying to push the men back. And they were all men today. Had they just been walking through the park? Or had they come to Laurelhurst on purpose?

Whichever, they were hell bent on spreading their petty hatred, and Charlie couldn't have it.

"Hail Thor!" he growled, then shoved a man to the ground.

"I've got your back!" Sean called.

"That's good!" Charlie shouted back, then got clocked on the forehead by a wild swing. He wrapped his arms around the man's skinny shoulders and flung him away from the ritual dance.

He couldn't stop them all, though. Some of the Nazis broke through, heading to the pole. Charlie ran that direction.

Children screamed. Men shouted. "This is white people's culture!" Charlie made out over the crash of sounds. What the...?

The drums stopped for a moment, then started up again.

A flying tackle caught him from behind, and he and a burly, bearded man wrestled each other to the ground. Charlie twisted, bucking his hips to throw the man off. He got enough distance to punch the man's jaw. That hurt. The man rolled all the way off him, holding his face and cursing.

C'mon, Thor. If you're here, help me out, will you?

He felt the buzzing that signaled the God's arrival, and a shot of adrenaline pumped through his body.

With a mighty roar, Charlie leapt back to his feet, and shoulder–to-shoulder with Joshua and the Sons of Ṣàngó, proceeded to beat the snot out of the assholes.

29

RAQUEL

The classroom and meeting space of the Inner Eye usually felt homey to Raquel, but today, the colorful Elemental Banners loomed over her on the walls. Air. Fire. Water. Earth. Each with their own color and pattern. The space behind the purple Celtic-knot-patterned door curtain felt way too crowded, and not everyone had arrived yet. She knew that part of this feeling was her own agitation, and part of it was that everyone was upset.

A damn room of empaths and psychics too upset to shield meant that the psychic space was both noisy and crowded with emotion. There was more space for bodies, but the psychic boundaries were already straining at the seams.

Raquel drummed her fingers on her arms, which were crossed over her chest. She'd thrown on her favorite orange hoodie, more for comfort than for warmth, and had even thrown her black leather jacket on over that. That jacket might be useful come nightfall, but right now? It was strictly an invocation of bad-assery and strength. A witch used whatever tools were at her disposal, including the ones that lived in her closet.

"Have some tea. You look like you need it." Selene handed Raquel a steaming mug that looked like straw-colored water and smelled like a combination of chamomile and mint.

"Thank you," Raquel said to her coven mate, who took one of the wooden chairs next to Raquel, sitting with a whoosh of black fabric and the slight clank from the metal bracelets currently skimming up their arms. Selene always looked just so. Arched eyebrows, ruby lip stain, pale skin, and long, straight black hair that complemented their usual black clothing.

Raquel sipped at the tea, wishing everyone would hurry the hell up and arrive so they could call this meeting to order.

She raised an eyebrow at Brenda, who was over at the pocket kitchen, refilling the electric kettle. Brenda shook her head and went back to what she was doing.

Raquel sighed. She knew she was being difficult, but she also had better things to do with her time than sit in this stew of emotions, waiting on a bunch of old hippies to find parking.

Not fair, Raquel. Get your own shit together. She chastised herself before her thoughts could spiral out of control. The Wyrd Sisters were Portland institutions, and had been working magic in the city for two decades. They were all powerhouses, and Arrow and Crescent Coven was going to need them.

Raquel began counting her breaths, in and out, stretching her inhalations and exhalations in the basic prac- tice she'd first learned when she started her magical practices all those years ago. It helped. The knots of tension in her shoulders and stomach muscles slowly uncoiled.

A couple of the Sons of Ṣàngó came trooping in the door to the back classroom space, looking around before they found seats. Shawn came over to greet her.

"How you doing, sister?"

"I'm okay. Pissed off, but okay. Thanks."

And distracted by her anger, and by the knowledge that her son was still at home, injured.

She had run home to check on Zion after the debacle in the park. Raquel was still shaking. She was *so* glad she hadn't let him come to the ritual. After feeding him some chicken soup she'd brought home from the café the day before, Raquel made sure he was all right. She also checked that yes, he had Jack's phone number in case he needed anything, she left again, grateful that Jack was home. As neighbors went, Jack was one of the best.

But she didn't like it. Not one bit. She'd almost asked the coven to meet at her house, but knew that a bunch of extra people were going to show up and that the classroom space at the Inner Eye would fit everyone more comfortably.

Besides, Zion didn't need more disruption in the home. He needed to lie back and read or watch videos, and let himself heal. She knew him: he would want to be part of the conversation, especially if the Sons of Ṣàngó were in the house.

Her baby wasn't such a baby anymore. He was halfway to a man, and fully invested. How could he not be? His mother had been beat down and so had he. The Black child that didn't know the terror of all that was lucky.

She just thanked the Gods they were both okay.

The scent of vetiver and rose preceded a chorus of voices. Finally. The Wyrd Sisters had arrived.

And Charlie walked in the room. Raquel didn't realize how much she needed to see him until he did.

Selene waved him over. "He can take my seat," they said.

"Thanks, Selene."

Charlie's brow was furrowed and beneath his jacket, his shirt and jeans were dirty from the melee in the park. There was a small bandage above his eyebrow. When he saw her, he smiled and his feet ate the floor in three big strides. Folding into the chair, he drew her into his arms, surrounding her with the scent of clean sweat, blackboard chalk, and sunshine.

"You okay?" he murmured into her ear.

She nodded into his shoulder, inhaling the scent of him for one more moment before pulling away.

"I'll do. You?"

"I've been better," he said, eyes looking a little tight around the edges.

Brenda cleared her throat from across the room, still stationed near the tea things, standing because every chair in the room was filled.

"So," she said, "I'll begin this meeting by asking each of us to find our center, and connect to that which we hold sacred."

The room drew in one collective breath, and the agitation that had been swirling through the air dissipated as people grounded themselves again. Thank Goddess Brenda was so skilled. A lesser priestess would never have reminded the group to center, would have launched right in to the meeting, ratcheting up the sense of unease.

"We thank the powers who travel with each person here. They are welcome in this space," Brenda continued, eyes closed. Then she opened her blue eyes, and stood a little taller and more firm. "We were all at the park today. We saw the fascists come in, disrupt our ritual, grab our sacred ribbons, and insist that we had stolen their traditions. This is dangerous magic they are working, whether they intend it or not. Their acts grow the thought forms that some people are lesser, and that racial purity and segregation should be our true ideals. Twice, they attacked our friend Charlie's shop, plus, they beat down Raquel *and* set their children to beat and threaten her son, Zion."

There were gasps around the room at that.

"So what are we going to do about it?" asked one of the Wyrd Sisters. Elspeth, her name was. A pretty, soft-bodied white woman in her early seventies, with cropped silver hair and a bright blue, flowing dress. Elspeth had been a rabble rouser her whole life, though the past few years she tended her garden more often than going toe to toe with the police.

"We need to organize," Shawn, from the Sons of Ṣàngó spoke. He was leaning against the wall near the purple door curtain. "We need to organize our magic. We need to call on our ancestors and deities to help us. And we need to figure out how to link together in a way that will feel solid and useful, rather than working at cross purposes."

"That's a tall order," Selene replied from their perch on the tall stool near Brenda.

"And who can we trust?" Moss asked. "I mean, look at us. We're Black, Latinx, Asian, old, queer.... And no offense, but the white heterosexuals here are mostly old hippies. None of us have a lot of currency with the overculture. Anyone who works with us? We're going to have to *know* they're solid. And we don't have the option to run to the cops with this, that's for sure."

"You speak the truth," Shawn replied. "And we do need to be careful. But trust is also necessary. We need to listen to the Powers and the Gods, and get ourselves as clean as possible inside so the guidance comes through clearly. I know we're all on edge, and we're going to want to rush into this, but we need to make certain that we act from our strengths, and not our weaknesses, and that we can draw upon each other, strength to strength."

Raquel grabbed at his words as if they were bread and she was hungry. She'd lost her connection to her power. Beneath her rage was fear and bewilderment. Fear for Zion. Fear for Charlie. Fear for the city that had raised her. How the hell was she supposed to get back to full power?

:Remember love.: Yemoja spoke inside her once again. She felt the rightness of the thought, but still wondered how.

Brenda sent her a sharp look, as if she saw the struggle going on inside Raquel. She probably did.

If I trust you, will you show me how? Raquel worried the smooth beach glass in her jacket pocket. A sense of well-being flowed into her. It was just a trickle, but enough to calm her. To lend her strength.

That was answer enough for now.

Raquel stood.

"My son is lying in bed now, with two cracked ribs and cuts and bruises from a terrible beating." She touched her own cheek. "My bruises are only now starting to fade from the punch I took from one of the white supremacists who is already back on the streets. Shawn is right. We need to organize our magic. Work together. But we also need to organize beyond this room. We're not going to face these men and women down with just ourselves and our magic."

"What are you suggesting?" Elspeth asked.

"We need to form a coalition. Not only the Gods, the ancestors, and whatever other magic workers we happen to trust. We need to work with the people who have been fighting fascism and terrorism all along. The Black militant groups. The anarchists. Antifa. The pro-immigration groups."

"Are they going to want to work with a bunch of witches?" one of the other Wyrd Sisters asked, looking up from her knitting.

"They've worked with us before," Moss replied.

"And they'll do so again," Raquel answered.

The feeling of strength inside her increased at the thought. That was good.

But she couldn't completely shake the unease. Not yet. There were too many variables. Too many moving parts.

Too many things that could go wrong.

30

CHARLIE

Charlie sat on the sofa in his dark living room, staring out the windows at the play of light and shadow outside. Staring at nothing, really, a local IPA in one hand, forgotten. Books of runes on the side table. Forgotten.

His mind replayed the skirmish in the park. And the meeting at Brenda's shop. And Zion's battered face. And the way Raquel felt in his arms.

What the hell had brought him here? To this place? Fighting fucking Nazis, for God's sake.

People like his father, it turned out. All of the little hints and comments over the years, the boxes full of who knows what in a house he needed to deal with as soon as things calmed down. *If* things calmed down.

They had to, right? No one could stay at war forever, not and live a life.

He shook his head. Of course people lived in war forever. There were children around the world who had never known a life outside of war. But Charlie could only barely imagine it. The thought was too terrible to bear.

"Dad, what the hell were you about? And who the hell are your cronies?"

And how had Charlie avoided thinking about it, all these years? He was sure Raquel would say that was his white privilege kicking in. Swaddled in that, a person didn't have to think about what built their actual circumstances. Racism? Eh, sure, Grandma Jane made some comments, but she was still a good person. She didn't actually *hate* anyone. Right?

Charlie was catching a glimpse of just how much love and caring and hatred had been intertwined in his family. Coming face to face with over-the-top racists like the Hack-Master Nazis and their friends? It highlighted just how much he'd always ignored. Even when Hai would tell him about some microagressions he got in the comic book community, Charlie still didn't get it.

Well, he was going to have to step up and start getting it now. Especially if he wanted Owlbear to remain a haven for every geeky child, teen, and adult who walked through its door. And especially if he wanted Zion and Raquel in his life. And he did.

Charlie wondered just how many friends he'd failed over the years, by not paying close enough attention.

His buzzer rang. Charlie walked through the dark living room and opened one of the side wall windows, the ones closest to the door. Poking his head out, he saw the familiar shape of Raquel's fall of dreads.

"Raquel!"

She looked up, face half in shadow, but all beautiful.

"I'll buzz you up."

What was she doing here? Charlie went to unlock and open the apartment door and switch on some lamps, throwing a warm glow around the bookshelves, wood floors, artwork, couch, and two chairs.

He heard her on the stairs, moving slowly, tread heavy. Damn. The woman must be exhausted. He turned just as she walked through the door and dropped her purse on the floor.

Charlie held out his arms. She walked straight into them. He held her lightly, breathing in the coffee scent of her, feeling her dreadlocks against his cheek and chin where she nestled her head.

"Hey."

"Hey."

They stood like that for the space of several heartbeats, before Raquel turned her face upward for a kiss.

That kiss was magic. Soft and firm. Sweet and urgent. The hoppy aftertaste of his beer met the tang of salt. Had she been crying? He pulled away.

"Where's Zion?"

"I called my mom to come sit with him. I left him alone too much today. Our neighbor, Jack, was looking in on him, but had to go out tonight."

"Come on. Let's sit."

Gently, he steered her toward the couch, and put an arm around her. She snuggled in close, head resting in the crook of his shoulder.

"Want to talk about it?"

She nodded, and wiped at her face. Charlie looked down. Her cheeks were wet.

"I know we have to do this, but I just want to run away. I mean, I'm furious, right? I want to tear those bastards limb from limb. But I don't trust that'll keep Zion safe, either. So that makes me want to run away. Get him someplace where this won't happen again."

She shifted on the couch, fishing in the pocket of her leather jacket. Dragging out a handkerchief, she blew her nose.

"But I don't know where would be any safer, you know?"

Charlie nodded, not trusting himself to speak. Not knowing the right words, but wanting to be there for her. He had so much to learn, and the revelations of the week had proven to him that love wasn't enough.

Not to be with someone like Raquel. And fuck, not even to be a real friend to Hai or Sam. He felt irritated with himself. Where the hell had he been all these years?

"What do you need?" he finally asked.

She moved again, so she could look him in the eyes. God, she looked so sad...but intent, too. She placed on hand on his cheek. It was cold as the ocean floor.

"Are you cold?" he asked.

"I want you to warm me up. It's...it's Beltane. It's Beltane, and I've had the worst week of my life, Nazis ruined my favorite ritual of the year, and Goddess, I just want to feel alive."

He bent his head toward hers. Raquel's lips opened. With gentle fingers, he wiped away her tears. She crawled up on his lap; his arms wrapped around her. He wanted to kiss her forever. Or as long as she would let him.

She broke her lips from his, and, forehead to forehead, eyes closed, whispered, "I want you to make love to me, Charlie."

"Are you sure?" he whispered back.

"Yes," she said.

Charlie wrapped her closer with one arm, and rocked forward on the couch. Wrapping the other arm around the curves of her hips, he stood. She twined her legs tight around his waist.

He carried her into his bedroom, and laid her sweet, lush body down.

31

RAQUEL

Raquel was in her bright kitchen, making hot chocolate for Zion, at his request.

She had stayed home from the café, needing to be near her son. Raquel's mother luckily could stay with Zion again in the evening, when Raquel needed to head to a planning meeting. It still felt strange, relying on her mother for help like this. In recent years, she'd grown used to not asking Mama for help. After Andy died, Raquel's mother had been great, but after a while, help had turned into wanting to control Raquel and Zion's life.

Mama meant well—it was all for love—but she could be a bit smothering. Raquel knew she would have swooped in and made it impossible for Raquel to do what she needed to do.

Raquel didn't have to worry about Andy's parents smothering anything. They saw Zion once a year, and Raquel still felt like, though they loved their grandson, he was also a painful reminder of what they had lost.

Even though Zion protested that he was fine, and didn't need a babysitter, Raquel could tell he was relieved

Grandma was coming. After the beating he'd taken, he needed way more mothering than usual.

She carefully stirred the milk and powdered chocolate, making sure it didn't burn or develop the disgusting skin along the top.

Raquel was feeling a little better, at least. Sex with Charlie had not only been wonderful, but had been just the thing to help heal her, body and soul. Because of Zion, she hadn't spent the night, but the two hours she'd spent away from home had felt luxurious. Her body still tingled from it.

Thank you, mother.

Yemoja liked her priestesses satisfied and happy. *Because she can push us harder that way,* Raquel thought, only half sarcastically.

She poured the chocolate into Zion's Avengers mug and walked down the hallway to his room. The white door was ajar, but she gave a rap on the frame before entering.

Zion's room smelled of boy and Tiger Balm. A cherry-wood student desk sat against the wall, under shelves teeming with books and action figures. Avengers posters graced the walls. The curtains to the one window were open to let in the May sun.

Raquel dragged the desk chair over to the twin bed where Zion stretched out beneath the Straight Outta Wakanda comforter she'd surprised him with for his birthday the month before. He looked a little better, but Raquel still fretted over him. She knew he was worried about her, too.

It had been just the two of them since Zion was four, going on five. Even before then, they hadn't seen much of Zion's dad, Andy. Andy had spent way too much of his precious time in Afghanistan, before losing his life to that IED. Raquel loved Andy, but her thirty-five-year-old self didn't have the same respect for the military that her twenty-something self had.

She'd never really had family with Andy. Not the "ride or die" relationship the songs talked about. But life with him had brought her Zion. She couldn't really ask for anything more. Other than to get these assholes to leave her son the hell alone.

"Did you go see Charlie last night?"

Oh boy. "Yes. Is that okay?"

He nodded. "I like him. He's always been cool to me, you know?"

Raquel did know, and it was one of the reasons she was letting herself fall for the tall blond man. She knew that, even before she'd ever even noticed him, he'd been kind to her son and his friends.

She just hoped...that it was all going to work out. Dating as a single parent was so tricky. You wanted your kid to like the people you dated, but also, you worried if they got too attached too soon. Zion already had a relationship with Charlie. That made some things easier, but she'd also need to keep an eye on things. Make sure the three of them didn't start doing too much together.

She didn't want Zion to start building a family with someone new until she was sure.

"Mom?"

"Yeah?"

"I keep feeling..." He screwed up his face, furrowing his brow. Thinking. "Like. You know how the coven talks sometimes about information 'wanting to come through'?"

The air changed in the room and Raquel stilled herself inside, every bit of her paying attention.

"Yes? What about it?" she asked gently.

"I keep feeling like there's pressure"—he gestured toward the center of his chest—"here."

"Does it hurt? It's not your ribs, is it?"

He shook his head, frustrated. "No. I mean, I think that's why I didn't notice it at first. Everything hurt too much. But now? It feels like something wants to talk to me or something. It's in my chest, but also, sometimes the back of my head feels a little buzzy."

"Where?"

He cupped a palm around the base of his skull, right where it met his spine. The classic entry point for spirits and the Powers. Shit.

"That definitely sounds like something's trying to come through," she said, carefully. "Do you want help closing it down? I can do that for you. It might help you rest."

"No," he said. "I want you to help me. Show me what you do when you need to listen."

She knew exactly what he was asking her. Every witch would. She had also known—sensitive as her boy was?—that this would come someday. But now? He was too young!

:You don't always get to choose when we arrive, daughter. I can help with this. Just ask.:

The taste of saltwater touched Raquel's tongue. Yemoja was with her.

Okay. She was still a priestess. She could do this. *They* could do this.

"Slow down your breathing. Just the way you've practiced."

Zion took in a long, slow breath, held it, then exhaled slowly. He closed his eyes, settling more deeply into his pillow. Raquel looked with her inner eye, and saw his aura settle, too, the field around him deepening just slightly.

Raquel couldn't "see" colors or anything, but she had the power to perceive shifts in energetic states. It came in useful.

"Okay," she said. "Now pay attention to your chest area, and the base of your skull. Feel whatever sensations are there. Take an even deeper breath, and as you exhale, imagine your energy fields softening. Ask 'Who's there?'"

His face intent, but more relaxed than it had been since the beating, Raquel felt him doing as she asked. It was palpable, a shift in pressure, similar to gently pressing at water in a pool with the palm of your hand, or the way wind resistance felt to a child doing hand dips and dives out a car window.

"Who's there?" he asked, voice strong.

With her inner ear, Raquel heard distant drumming, just as she had in the park. She tensed, feeling the Powers draw near.

"Who is it, Zion?"

"Ṣàngó."

:He will help Zion, just as I help you.:

Zion's body gave a shudder as muscles contracted, then relaxed. The planes of his face adjusted, just slightly, round cheeks flattening, jaw growing more defined. He looked older than thirteen, especially to a mother's eyes.

Then Zion spoke, in a voice that was his and not his. It was deeper. Stronger. Older. Yet still her little boy's. The small hairs at the back of Raquel's neck prickled. She stopped herself from grabbing his hand. A sudden touch right now could jerk him back from his altered state, too quickly and too soon.

"I am that which rolls across vast distances, bringing thunder, and lightning, illuminating evil deeds, striking fear into the oppressors, and bringing light to those who await justice."

Zion's hands struck the comforter three times.

"The future shall lead us, crushing the moldering past beneath its heel. From the corners of the earth they come, a mighty war band. To strike fear in the hearts of those who desecrate the ways of old and poison that which is to come. The Powers of the Mighty walk this earth again, and we shall triumph, but only if the people shall believe."

The sense of ocean grew stronger in Raquel. It steadied her. Calmed her. The gibbering, angry, mother part of her, the part that only wanted her little boy to be happy, and safe, and protected from the evils of the world? It was still there, but it knew that to protect her son, Zion needed her to meet him as a witch.

"What else do you need to tell us, Mighty One?" she asked.

Zion's eyes snapped open. He turned his head and stared at her. His dark eyes burned like fire.

"Do what is necessary, and no more. Stand firm. Gather your forces. Strike swift and strong." Zion panted a little, as though holding the Power was growing to be too much effort. "And listen to my sister. She holds the other part."

Zion's face went slack, and a great, rattling, hissing breath expelled itself from his lungs. His cheeks grew round again, though his skin was tinged with gray. He blinked. Ran his hands across the comforter.

"Mom?"

She reached for him, gathering him into her arms, careful of his injured ribs, inhaling the scent of Tiger Balm and boy.

"Yes?"

"That was really weird."

She patted his back and dragged some pillows up,

helping him settle back into a half-seated position on the bed.

"It was weird. Powerful, too. Do you want to talk about it?"

He thought for a moment. "Not right now. I think...it needs to just *be* for a little bit. Does that make sense?"

She nodded. It did make sense. He needed to let the experience settle first. Get some distance. Turn it over in his mind. She was sure they had a lot of conversations in their future.

Looking down, she saw that skin had formed on the hot chocolate. Damn. He never got to drink it.

She kissed his forehead, then picked up the mug and stood. "I'm going to throw this out and make some more. Sound good?"

He nodded. She could tell he was exhausted. She paused at the doorway.

"Oh, baby. I feel like I should stay here with you."

His grave eyes held steady on her own.

"You heard what Ṣàngó said, Mom. You need to let everyone know. Besides..." He forced out a little smile. Her brave and beautiful son, trying to reassure her. "Grandma will bring my favorite Thai soup and she promised me a new video game."

"Okay, little man. I'm going to make this hot chocolate, then get changed. You need anything else?"

"I've got my comic books, Netflix, and don't have to do homework," he said. "I'm good."

And he'd just had an ancient Power speak through him. Raquel shook her head. He was good, her bright and shining son. Too good for this world sometimes.

She wasn't sure the world deserved him.

32

CHARLIE

Owlbear was full. Charlie and Sam had folded up the gaming tables to make more space, and Tempest had brought chairs over from the Inner Eye. Brenda was minding the shop, she had said. As a shop owner, Charlie understood for sure, but he would have liked Brenda's calming presence all the same.

Charlie stood just behind the counter, making sure there wasn't any trouble. Sam was near the door.

So far, it felt as though the protective runes were holding. Not that Charlie was an expert, or sanguine about anything right now, but it at least *felt* like the shop was being protected. That was all he could ask for right now. Just to not feel as if everything he cared about was under attack.

Speaking of a person he cared about... Raquel walked in, causing his breath to catch as he looked at her. Sam gave her a quick hug. Raquel looked worried and a little tired, but better than she had in a few days. That was good. Charlie rounded the counter and walked toward her as she moved into his arms for a quick hug. He brushed a kiss across her lips. Neither the hug or the kiss were enough. But considering they were heading into a war council, it would have to be enough.

"Good to see you," he said. "Zion okay?"

She sighed in response, and gave a little shake of her head. "He's actually doing pretty well, considering. But things are getting weirder and weirder, let me tell you."

He raised an eyebrow.

"I...can't right now," Raquel replied. "It's too complicated. But you'll hear some of it tonight."

"Okay," he said, giving her arms a small squeeze.

"I've got to go check in with the coven." She kissed him one more time and walked toward the clump of Arrow and Crescent witches who were having a private conversation over by the board game displays.

More and more people filtered in through the front door. Charlie was starting to wish he'd disabled the phaser sound for the night. Oh well. Too late now.

A tall, burly white man with a thick brown beard held out his hand. "I'm Tim. From Oak and Ash Kindred."

"Charlie." He clasped the man's hand, feeling a sense of recognition. Huh. Charlie didn't know what that meant. "Thanks for coming. There are still a few seats left on the other side of the room."

The man nodded and threaded his bulk through small clumps of people.

The Sons of Ṣàngó were already here. So were the older, hippie witches. What looked like a small crew of anarchists came in, wearing ragged black trousers and T-shirts. They were followed by a couple of folks that Sam said were from a local communist collective.

The geek squad was, of course, out in force.

Mostly, there were a handful of representatives from each group, just as they'd asked. At such short notice, not only was it impossible for everyone to make it, there was no one place to meet that was large enough for all the groups that needed to coordinate. If they'd wanted to wait another week or two, they likely could have gotten the union hall or a church basement, but when he'd spoken with Raquel on the phone earlier in the day, she said that several coven members were having bad psychic hits and needed to move on the situation, and move now. Charlie couldn't blame them. He wanted this done.

Besides, it seemed crystal clear that the white supremacists were escalating at every turn, and quickly. Word had just gone out today that another "Portland Patriots" meeting was scheduled for the coming weekend. They were just waiting on the location to be confirmed.

Sam looked at him, questioning. Charlie scanned the room and nodded for her to go ahead and lock the door. Pretty much every chair was full. If more folks showed up later, they could let them in. But no way was he leaving the door unlocked to let whatever white supremacists might be roaming the streets crash this party.

One of the anarchists, a young black man with a scruffy beard and retro flattop fade was passing around a big metal bowl. "Please power all your phones and other devices down and put them in the bowl."

"But I need my phone to take notes!"

"We brought paper," said one of the communists, sending a small stack of notepads and pens around the room.

Alejandro stood. "Tariq is right. We know that these white supremacists and Nazis have hackers. We also know the US government spies on activists, and there are some vulnerable communities here. Anything with a camera or microphone can be used to spy on us. I hate to sound paranoid, but trust me, I've been an IT geek for a lot of years, and I know what's what regarding computer security."

People still grumbled, but they powered down their phones and tablets and dropped them in the metal bowl.

"What about laptop computers?" That came from one of the Wyrd Sisters. Charlie couldn't keep track of everyone's names, so he was going for affiliations.

"Power them down, please," Tariq said. "They won't fit in the bowl but we can at least take them to another part of the space."

"They can go in the storeroom," Sam said. "Lots of metal in there to confuse any signals."

Tariq looked relieved.

Damn. Dude must be stressed all the time. Charlie was only just now getting a hint of what that must be like. To feel threatened all the time.

Sam and Tariq gathered all the tech and she let them into the storeroom.

"Okay, folks!" That was Moss. Calling the meeting to order. "Thank you all for coming. I'm Moss from Arrow and Crescent Coven. We're all here tonight because, as you know, there have been multiple attacks on our community in the past week, all by groups of white supremacists and Nazis."

The room quieted down. Folks shifted in their chairs and then settled. Ready to listen.

Charlie stood at attention, standing between the gaming room and the rest of the shop, not quite able to relinquish a position with clear access to the front door. He itched all over, every nerve on high alert.

Moss signaled to Lucy, who stood and took over.

"We know that some of you aren't used to working with witches or magic, and that others of you"—Lucy looked around the diverse crowd—"worked with us to save the Open Heart encampment in February. What Arrow and Crescent wants all of you to know is that we are not the leaders of this coalition, but we *will* be working magic. We hope you are all okay with that. And while I don't want to take up a lot of our precious meeting time explaining things, on every break members of Arrow and Crescent and our allies the Wyrd Sisters will be available to answer questions. Witches, could you all raise your hands please?"

Seventeen hands raised in the air. The rest of the room looked around, identifying the witches.

The air hummed. Charlie could tell this was a big moment. The witches all outing themselves and the non-witches, simply by remaining, tacitly agreeing to work with a bunch of shit they might not understand.

Charlie guessed that was what his couple of activist friends meant when they talked about diversity of tactics.

"Tariq?" Moss said.

Tariq stepped forward so more of the room could see him. He'd been standing near the storeroom with Sam.

"Peace. Thank you all for coming, comrades. I'm Tariq from the Lovers of the White Rose collective. LWR are anarchist anti-fascists, working in Portland, Beaverton, Gresham, and Vancouver. We'd like to talk to you all about possible organizing tactics and staying safe in the streets, and then we'll turn it over to Patricia from the Red Emma Collective and she'll talk to us about affinity groups and how they can operate in the sort of action we're planning this week. Cool?"

People nodded, and answered in the affirmative.

"Tariq?" Raquel said.

She had risen from her chair, and stood, clearly ready to speak.

"Yes, Raquel?"

"Before we start the rest of this meeting, I have a message my son, Zion, asked me to give to the group. It felt important to do it now." She swept her eyes around the room, standing a little taller. Charlie could almost feel when the mother and the priestess merged. The air practically crackled around her.

Charlie snapped back into a martial arts stance. He could feel the strange energy rising. Thor. The power slid through his muscles and kissed his veins.

"This message comes from Ṣàngó, the òrìṣà of lightning and war."

Charlie looked, and sure enough, Shawn and all the other Sons of Ṣàngó rose en masse. It was spooky. And pretty damn cool.

"As some of you know, Zion was badly beaten by the children of the same people that did this to me." She gestured to her cheek, which, though it had faded, was still obviously bruised. "Ṣàngó spoke through my son tonight. He wanted to let us all know that we were to gather our forces and strike swift and strong."

"What else, sister?" Shawn asked, staring at her so intently Charlie was surprised his eyes didn't burn a hole in her head.

She paused for a moment, as though listening, or searching her mind.

"He wanted us to know that these people are twisting the old ways, and that the new ways will triumph, restoring honor to the old."

"What do you think that means, though?" Tariq asked.

Charlie's muscles clenched as he saw the gaze she turned on the younger man. It was as if Raquel wasn't all the way there. And Charlie wasn't sure what was speaking in her place.

"It means that the young shall lead the old and crush that which would destroy the promise of the future. It means that we shall rise like a mighty wave, lit up by lightning, cresting on the shore."

Her words hung in the air. No one spoke, or even moved. Charlie stopped breathing.

"It means that we shall fuck shit up. With love. And strength. And righteousness. And that some of us may fall."

Charlie drew in a ragged breath.

Damn it. He could have done without that final sentence.

You're a fool, man, he thought. *After all these years, living with Dad, you forgot there's always a cost to be paid for war?*

He just hoped it wasn't too high.

33

———

RAQUEL

Raquel, Zion, and Charlie walked west across the Hawthorne Bridge. It was the Saturday after Beltane, another sunny, perfect spring day on the Willamette River. Charlie had found a little parking lot near the water fire station on the east side. That way, if things got clogged up because of the crowds, they would still be able to get the car out.

Their ad hoc committee to fight fascism didn't even have to coordinate a standoff. The Nazis had done that for them.

Turned out that the "Portland Patriots" rally was being held at the small park right on the river, between the Hawthorne and Morrison bridges. Sun glinted on the metal spans, and dragon boat teams practiced on the water down below. It would have been a gorgeous day to be heading toward the waterfront park, if only there weren't a bunch of assholes waiting.

It had been a huge week of planning, meetings, and organizing. Many more groups had signed on once they discovered what was going down, including a lot of the interfaith group the coven had worked with before, and some of the Black churches from Northeast Portland.

Mama, protect us all, she thought.

Raquel felt a little angry, a little frightened, but also pretty much invincible. Though that last was hubris, and she knew it. She was in full on priestess-warrior-witch mode. It was the only thing that was going to get her through this day.

Charlie reached out and took her hand. The connection reassured her. She gave his fingers a squeeze and dropped his hand again.

They weren't quite in the "displays of affection in front of Zion" stage of their relationship. Yet. But oh, she craved Charlie's touch. It had already been quite the day.

The morning had started with a huge fight. She insisted that Zion remain at home, safe, tending his still-sore ribs. He had thrown Ṣàngó's words back in her face, wanting to go. The sense Raquel got from Yemoja was that she agreed. Raquel knew when she was outvoted, and finally acquiesced. They'd worked out several different scenarios that would enable Zion to get out if necessary. A call to Alejandro had extracted the promise to watch out for the boy and take him to safety if shit really started to go down.

Zion trusted Alejandro with his life. She did, too, though she hoped that trust would prove unnecessary.

Zion had wanted to stick with her, but Raquel had a strong feeling that she herself would be otherwise preoccupied. Not the first choice she would make as a parent, but occasionally the priestess held sway.

"Do you see them?" she asked Zion.

"Yeah." He stretched a skinny arm out and pointed past the fountain courtyard down below, toward a grassy space just beyond a copse of blooming cherry trees. "It looks like people are gathering over there. I see an American flag."

"Good. Let's find the rest of the coven and hook up."

They walked down the offramp, heading into downtown.

Every group was meeting in a different spot off site, each of them only a few blocks away, so they had critical mass when they arrived at the park. The plan was to coordinate and then start marching at the same time. That way they should arrive at the waterfront simultaneously.

Arrow and Crescent, the Wyrd Sisters, and Oak and Ash Heathen Kindred had agreed to meet under the statue of Portlandia, to ask for her blessing. It was six blocks up from the river, so slightly farther than some of the other groups, but they would station themselves closer once their offerings were done.

It looked as if they were the last ones to arrive. A group of around twenty-five people clustered on the sidewalk in front of the fifteen-story, off-white stucco building with its terra cotta plinths. As impressive as the Deco-influenced, post-modern building was, Raquel barely noticed it. All it took was a glance up, and there was the glory of Portlandia herself.

Crouching on one powerful bronze knee, with a massive flow of hair, the statue of Portlandia blessed everyone who walked by.

Elspeth waved them over, her long gray hair braided tightly for once. She wore combat boots, as did most of the other Wyrd Sisters. The crones were ready for battle.

"We brought mead." Tim, a khaki jacket straining over his huge shoulders, hoisted an orangey-brown glass bottle that caught the sun.

"It's good to see you," Raquel said, giving him a one-armed hug, nodding at the other members of his kindred.

"Everyone who hasn't met him, this is Charlie. Charlie, this is everyone," she said.

She left Charlie to introduce himself, and led Zion over to Alejandro.

"You're good to keep track of each other today?" she asked. "And you have each other's phone numbers programmed in, right?"

Zion and Alejandro both nodded.

"We'll be fine," Alejandro reassured her. "No matter what happens, I won't let him out of my sight."

Raquel was still a little concerned. But she needed the backup and had it. Basically, if Yemoja came through full force, Raquel knew she needed to let that happen today. Or if Charlie needed backup...or any number of things.

Brenda walked over and gave her a deep hug. "Zion will be fine, Raquel."

"Promise?"

"Promise," her best friend said.

That actually made Raquel feel a little better, even if she still didn't like it. If Brenda had gotten a psychic hit otherwise, she would have told Raquel and they would have gotten Zion out of there.

Sometimes, you just had to trust the Powers. This was one of those days.

"Okay. Let's do this."

They turned back to the ragtag group of heathens and witches and formed an arc on the sidewalk.

Raquel took a breath, and imagined her energy connecting to the energy below, in the earth that rested deep beneath the city infrastructure. She felt the river, and the power of Yemoja in the water. She felt Zion. And Charlie.

Ṣàngó and Thor. What a strange grouping they all were. But they could work together, at least for today.

"Hail Portlandia!" Tim bellowed toward the sky. He raised the bottle, toasting toward the massive statue.

"Hail!" their little group responded.

"We ask that you guard this city, and keep your people safe from harm. We ask that you fill us with courage, and steadfastness. Guide us. Be with us. Portlandia, we honor you!"

He poured a measure of mead onto the little square of earth surrounding one of the sidewalk trees, then passed the bottle to the next person.

Each person, one by one, said a silent prayer, raised the bottle, and took a sip of mead.

When it got to Raquel, who was at the opposite end of the little arc, she centered herself, closed her eyes, and breathed.

Portlandia...keep my son safe. Watch over him today. And help us turn the tide in this city from hatred and intolerance to love and support. Thank you.

She lifted the bottle, looking up at one large, bronze eye. She swore the statue blinked. Raquel held the bottle to her lips, tasting the sweet honey wine, then walked the bottle back over to Tim.

Together, they poured the rest of the liquid onto earth.

"We give thanks," Tim said. "Okay. Everyone ready?"

Raquel was as ready as she was going to be. She just hoped she was ready enough.

There was no telling what exactly was to come.

34

CHARLIE

Charlie was in way over his head. Here he was, surrounded by actual activists, actual witches, and heathens who actually worked with runes. And Charlie? He was just a big geek who looked like Chris Hemsworth and, embarrassingly, turned out to have a weird affinity for Thor.

So far, the plan had come together seamlessly. All the disparate groups had streamed together into one mass of about—amazingly—eight hundred, that had marched down Naito Parkway toward this waterfront park, where they formed a human cordon around the Portland Patriots and the line of cops in riot gear who stood between both groups. The white supremacists were closest to the water.

"Look at those assholes," Hai said.

He and Sam flanked Charlie and Tim. Geeks and heathens mixing on the grass. The Wyrd Sisters, Sons of Sàngó, Xena, and Arrow and Crescent were intermixed with the larger crowd, just as they'd discussed in the planning meetings. They needed trusted point people interspersed among the random folks who had just showed up. The hope was that this would help with coordination if shit went down.

"The Nazis or the police?" Sam asked. She had her black hood pulled up today, despite the sun. Princess Leia looked tough as nails on the back.

"Both," Hai replied.

Charlie noticed that the police faced outward, away from the white supremacists, and toward the hippies and anarchists. They were in full riot gear. Helmets. Shields. Batons. Some had what looked like rifles with orange stocks. He supposed they were for "less than lethals" that could still result in terrible injuries.

The park was filled with shouting people. The "patriots" had a small sound system and an actual mic. One of them was droning on about keeping America strong and its people safe. Folks on the other side of the police line hurled insults back at them, and a group of Black pastors and other interfaith folks prayed out loud. He saw Tariq from Lovers of the White Rose, gesticulating at a small group of his comrades.

The Snack Bloc was set up on the edges of the park, handing out ice cream, protein bars, and bottles of water.

It was quite the mix of sound and fury. Charlie wished he could just enjoy this strange slice of Portland on this beautiful day. Unfortunately, there was work to be done. Now, if only he knew how to do it.

"Tim!" Charlie called to the large heathen.

"What's up, man?" Tim passed a hand over his lush brown beard.

"I'm...this sounds weird, but Thor is..."

"Just spit it out, I guarantee you I've heard weirder shit before."

Charlie allowed himself to sag in relief, just for a moment, before breathing steel back into his spine.

"Thor has asked me to help protect my people. This is all new to me, but some of the witches say he's actually been...speaking through me. And he wants me to draw a rune ring around our group, to keep them safe from these assholes, kind of the way the cops are keeping the assholes safe."

"And you want help?"

"Yes."

"You got it man. Let's start."

"Watch our backs?" Charlie said to Hai and Sam.

Then both men turned away from the cops and toward the teeming crowd. It was truly huge. Charlie had no idea how they were going to do it.

He turned to his left. All of a sudden, Raquel was right there. Where had she come from? She gave him a kiss. He closed his eyes and inhaled her for a moment, memorizing the press of breasts and lush, round hips, her coffee smell, and the taste of her lips.

She leaned away from him, and looked into his eyes. "You got this."

He gave a tight nod, turned to Tim, and said "What now?"

"Now we chant the runes, my friend. You ever done that before?"

"Nope."

Tim gave a wild grin.

"Well then. Today's the day! Just follow my lead." Tim turned his head. "Hai and Sam? You ready??"

"Sure thing," Hai replied.

Tim turned to the north, clasped his hands together, and

traced a hammer shape in the air. Then he began chanting, starting with the first letter of the alphabet, the rune fehu.

"Fehu, fehu, fehuuuuu." Tim's voice rumbled outward across the grass, the trees, and the people.

Charlie tried to match Tim's tone, "Fehu, fehu, fehuuuu."

He felt the buzzing at his skull as the rune rolled from his mouth. Charlie imagined it shining on the other side of the crowd, an upward tilted F, beginning the ring that would offer protection to the crowd.

They chanted the rune three times, then moved on to the next.

Uruz. The wild aurochs. Strength. Pure, primal power.

Charlie widened his stance, took in a deep breath, and blended his voice with Tim's.

"Uruz, uruz, uuurruuuz."

Syllable by syllable, rune by rune, with the power of the sky and earth, and the buzzing at the base of Charlie's skull, they built the ring.

35

———

RAQUEL

Raquel left Charlie and Tim to their work. She had her own to do.

Surrounded by the churning crowd, she found a small patch of grass, and rooted her energy more deeply in the ground beneath her feet. The earth held and supported her. She let her witch self rise up inside of her, pulling on the power of the river, tracing its pathway north, to where it flowed into the Columbia, and further, to where the Columbia kissed the Pacific.

"Yemọja," she whispered, the word drowned in the noises of the crowd. "Yemọja. River. Ocean. Mother. Lover. Power. Be with me now. Be with us all."

She felt a tingling along her skin as the power of water flowed into her body. Raquel licked her lips and opened out her arms.

Closing her eyes for a moment, she felt the strength of the crowd, the push and pull of them. The battering from in front and from behind. She let the noise and the heat of it wash around her, as if she were a stone in the midst of a river of humanity.

Taking a moment, she scanned the crowd, trying to see if Zion was still there. A movement in one of the trees further back toward the sidewalk caught her attention. And there he was, grinning, waving from among the branches of a cherry tree. Surrounded by pale pink blossoms, he looked happy for the first time in weeks.

She could just make out Alejandro's head. Her coven mate stood beneath the tree, arms crossed over his chest. He looked ready for anything.

Thank you, mother, for my coven. For my life.

Zion bent his head down, saying something to Alejandro. Then someone passed up a mic attached to a bullhorn with a black coil—was that Tariq?—and all of a sudden, Zion was speaking, voice just carrying over the sounds of the crowd.

"Remember who you are!" he said. "Remember what you're fighting for!"

Holy shit. What the hell was Zion doing?

Raquel formed her shoulders into a wedge, and tried pushing her way through the crowd. But it was too dense. She couldn't fight her way through.

"Damn it!" she said. "Mother! Help me!"

:You must let him work his will.:

"No! He's just a *boy!*"

"Ouch! Watch it, lady!"

Raquel didn't even notice the person she'd just stepped on. Panic rose inside her. She had to get to her son.

"The drums of war only beat when there is a thing worth fighting for," Zion continued. The bullhorn squeaked and crackled, but his voice came through, true and clear. "Make certain you know, in your heart, what you are fighting *for*, not just what you fight *against*."

The crowd stilled for a moment, drinking in Zion's

words. *Ṣàngó*'s words. The reason Zion had insisted on coming out today.

:Listen.:

Raquel *was* listening now. Every bit of her paid close attention. The words penetrated, striking home. She was fighting for Zion. She fought for his future. For the future of every Black, geeky boy and girl.

She came to a dead stop and raised her fist in the air. Up in the cherry tree, Zion raised his own, mirroring her salute.

A crew of drummers had shown up, and began pounding out a rhythm at the back of the crowd, toward Naito Parkway and the trees. Raquel danced a little, eyes still on Zion, catching the beat and using it to fuel the magic flowing through her body.

"Let the drums of the ancestors call us home!" Zion said. "Fight for love! Fight for justice! Fight for beauty! Fight for righteousness! Fight for the future!"

That was most certainly not her son speaking. But she had to trust that Alejandro would help him out of the tree when the time came. And that her coven mate would also help Zion come back from whatever place allowed him to access the ancient Powers.

Ancestors, watch over my son. Protect him, mama. You, too, Ṣàngó.

Then, deciding to trust in the Powers, she blew Zion a kiss, turned around, and began to wade back to the front lines.

:Stop.:

"What?" Raquel looked around, scanning for danger. She felt the row of riot cops behind her, toward the river, facing the people protesting the Nazis, of course. The cops never seemed to go up against the white supremacists themselves. Too many supporters in their ranks.

She felt the white supremacists behind the cops, a roiling mass of seething hatred, interspersed with pockets of glee, and a few people that actually felt earnest. Whatever.

She felt the anger, fear, and outrage of the people between her and the sidewalk. *Her* people. The ones who had planned and coordinated, and come together to face the danger and hatred infecting their city. Raquel reached even further, sending the sense of river water rippling outward, connecting her people to the support, power, and flow of Mama Yemoja.

Raquel could sense the members of Arrow and Crescent as the water washed around them. The Wyrd Sisters. The heathens. Antifa. A few of the local Black churches. An immigrants' support group. All the different people they'd reached out to over the past week, who had gathered themselves together on this piece of sacred ground, once walked only by the Multnomah. She offered a quick prayer of thanks to the first peoples of this land.

The drummers segued into Ṣàngó's rhythm. Was that good, or bad? She felt the Sons of Ṣàngó, all heading toward the street. Craning to see between the bodies surrounding her, she caught sight of the fighters, dressed in white and red, running past Zion's tree. Why?

And then she felt it. The discordance. The glee. The hatred. It was no longer just near the river. It was at the street.

Just beyond Charlie and Tim's ring of power, they were surrounded by white supremacists. Shit.

The crowd around her roared and began to chant.

CHARLIE

"Ban-ish Na-zis! Ban-ish hate!"

The crowd started chanting. Right after Tim and Charlie had gotten the rune ring up, Zion began speaking from a perch in a cherry tree. Some powerful and kind of spooky words to be coming from such a young person.

Charlie guessed he needed to get used to a lot of powerful and spooky things. Like the runes he could sense flickering around the crowd. They were palpable, practically humming in the back of his mind. It felt as if he could reach out and pluck them from the sky. Tim knew what he was doing.

In the building of the ring, Charlie had lost track of Raquel. He really hoped she was okay.

The crowd pushed toward the ring of cops and the white supremacists behind them. The helmeted police smacked their batons against riot shields, warning off the crowd.

"Stop protecting fascists!" someone behind him shouted. A bottle sailed overhead and hit one of the polycarbonate shields with a splat of cheap plastic, spewing water everywhere. The cops surged forward, shoving at the crowd with their shields.

In the midst of the confusion, Charlie heard the sound of drums.

He struggled to maintain focus. Struggled to keep the rune ring up around the crowd. It began to flicker in and out.

"Tim!" he shouted.

"Ban-ish Na-zis! Ban-ish hate!"

The big man clamped a hand on his shoulder, and leaned in close. "I'm right here. Hold it steady, man!"

Charlie tried. He really tried.

Thor? If you're real, and you're around? We could really use your help, man.

The strange, buzzing feeling was back. Charlie felt the runes around the crowd strengthen, crackling and humming, pulsating in counterpoint to the rhythm of the drums.

He smelled the grass, the river, and the rising sweat of a hyped-up crowd.

Charlie, left hand on Tim, right hand raised into the air, began to rotate his arm in a clockwise fashion, following the trajectory of the twenty-four shapes that glowed and glimmered, shining red in his mind's eye.

Right. Red.

"Tim? You got a knife?"

"Yeah, man."

"Cut me."

Tim didn't hesitate for a moment. Just fished in his pocket and snapped a pocketknife open. Charlie offered him his right hand. Tim slashed a small stripe on the fleshy part of his pointer finger. Red beaded up right away.

Tim slashed the pointer finger on his own left hand, then looked at Charlie.

"My blood's okay," he said. "Yours?"

Charlie nodded. "Got tested six months ago. I'm good. What...?"

Tim nodded, pressed his finger to Charlie's, just for a moment, then Charlie's hand with his own.

Both men raised their fists this time. Charlie felt the warmth of Tim's huge palm, the sting of the cut, and the wet of the blood as it ran through his clenched fist and down his arm.

He felt the change when a drop of blood hit the ground. The power of it *boomed* around him, rippling outward, causing the cops to stagger and the drums to falter, just for a moment. Tim gripped his hand harder.

The crowd paused for one breath, and the chanting started up again.

Then everyone rushed toward the street.

Charlie and Tim were caught up in the crowd, being pulled and shoved along.

"Hold on to the ring!" Tim shouted.

Tim slammed into Charlie's shoulder and fell, dragging at Charlie, who dropped his hand. A stupid Nazi prick grinned, then shook his hand out and ran. He'd punched Tim, who rolled on the ground, holding his ears.

How the hell had he gotten through the rune ring? It felt so solid!

"Fuck!" Charlie shouted. "Tim!" He crouched over the big man, trying to protect him from the running crowd. Trying to keep that damn rune ring up. He felt Thor knocking at the back of his head, telling him to stand.

So he did. Charlie straddled Tim, one foot on either side of his torso, and spread his arms out wide, making space.

The crowd eddied around the two men. The ring of runes still held.

Thank God, Charlie thought. One in particular. *Thanks, Thor.*

The effort of holding the ring in the midst of the barrage spiked a sharp pain through his skull. Gritting his teeth, Charlie stood as tall and steady as he could.

He just hoped the witches were doing better than he was. And he hoped Raquel and Zion were both safe.

"Sam! Hai!" Charlie needed backup now that Tim was down.

"Here! What do you need?" Hai's eyes were intense, and Sam looked practically feral.

"Help me protect Tim! I can't do that and hold the ring up myself!"

As the words left his mouth, three floppy-haired white men ran toward them. Fuckers. It was Blond No Socks and Dark Haired dude, plus some other jackass. The Hack-Master assholes from the store. Charlie swung his hand and punched the blond one in the face. No Socks squealed in rage. Charlie's hand throbbed in pain, then his head snapped back from the return blow. He tasted blood.

And saw the SS runes on the asshole's jacket.

Rage joined the spiking pain in Charlie's head. The rune ring wobbled as he snapped an uppercut into the man's jaw. He couldn't fight and focus on the runes. He almost tripped over Tim. Damn it.

Charlie sensed Sam and Hai, fighting off their assailants alongside him. Heard the crunch of bone, and the grunts and pants of effort. He smelled spit, anger, and... kerosene?

And fire. Holy fucking Gods, was something on fire?

White hot pain crawled up his back.

He whirled, only to see another grinning white man, whipcord thin, waving his fingers in his face.

"Charlie!" Sam screamed, then began beating at his back. "Your back is on fire!"

Searing heat licked at his jeans. He looked down. The bastard had dumped kerosene on Tim's legs, then threw a match. Charlie dropped hard onto Tim's legs, then rolled, trying to put out the flames on Tim's legs and his back at the same time.

A fist connected with his left temple. A blow from behind.

Bastards...

Everything went black.

37

RAQUEL

Raquel ran toward the rest of her coven. Arrow and Crescent had formed a half moon, arms linked together. Alejandro was the only one missing.

"Did..." She could barely form a sentence over the shouting, and drumming, and the pushing, angry panic all around them. It was hard to think.

"Zion's safe," Brenda replied. "Moss and Lucy helped Alejandro get him out before this end got blocked in. They barely made it back in time."

"But we're here now, ready to smite these pendejos," Lucy said, dark hair bound tightly behind her, face fierce and grim.

"Okay. We ready?"

The other seven members of Arrow and Crescent all nodded.

"You're lead today, sister," Selene said.

Raquel felt tears pricking at her eyes. She loved these people so much. Almost as much as Zion. She closed her eyes and sent up a quick prayer for his protection, and Charlie's too, then took in a deep breath of grass- and sweat-scented air. There was an undertone of kerosene and a tickling at the back of her head that bothered her. But she couldn't trace either of them well enough to figure out what was going on.

Focus, girl.

Raquel centered herself. Reached for the earth beneath her. Felt her coven around her. The river behind her. The cops and the patriots in between. Charlie? She felt confusion there, then nothing.

She re-centered, took another breath, and reached, answered by the power of Yemọja and Ṣàngó. They were there. Stronger than ever. She just hoped she was strong enough. Much as she tried shoving her doubts away, there they were, a presence in the midst of her need to be strong. To get this done.

So much hinged on her doing what she used to do best. Being a priestess and witch.

Unlike some of the other actions the coven had done in concert with other local activists, this one required the coven to make the magic, and everyone else to provide energy, protection, and distraction.

Every day a new day. Every action a new action. Each piece of magic, something that had never been seen before.

No matter how many times you repeated a thing, it was new. Maybe she could be new, too?

"Raquel?" That was Brenda again, asking her what the hell she was waiting for.

Raquel took a deep breath.

"I'm ready now," she said. She would have to be.

"Everybody, link!" Brenda called out.

Raquel felt the energy of each coven member move through the arc, twining together in the strange marriage they made when they worked together. Family. Joined beyond blood and breath, linked in the æthers, in all the planes from above to below and beyond.

She moved her feet, stomping softly on the ground, finding the rhythm. Finding the source of the dance.

She felt the ring of runes that still surrounded them. Felt it waver, then flare, crumbling to the ground, sucking away some of the power of the crowd with it. Shit. Was the protection ring gone now? Some residue of power still flickered in her mind's eye. Not enough. Damn.

She really hoped Charlie was okay, but there was no time to do anything about it.

"Okay, Raquel. What next?" she said out loud.

What next?

Her aura flashed, and fire and water crashed within her, threatening to drown her, burn her, stretch her molecules so far they disintegrated.

Nooooooo, she roared inside her head, roaring at the Powers that fought to take her over. She fought against it. Fought to bring herself back into control. *My name is Raquel Melissa Bradford! I am a priestess! A mother! A witch! I call upon you now to work* with *me and* through *me.*

The fire and water formed a mighty braid of creation. Thunder and lightning rumbled and flashed, despite the clear, sunny day. The scent of the river filled her nose and mouth, almost choking her. Gasping for breath, she tasted the sweetness of the cherry blossoms, and felt the longing within each gathered heart.

Still fighting to regain her own power, she wrestled with the òrìṣà, finally recalibrating her energies with theirs. Fire and water clicked in, joining her Raquel-ness. Linking with the person she was at her core. The woman she'd been running from for the past few years. The woman who *knew* how to raise and protect her son. The woman who *knew* she was desirable, and worthy of love. The woman who could dance with the Gods and face Nazis and cops, any damn day of the week.

It felt good. Necessary. Right.

Raquel took in a mighty breath, and stamped her feet in the rhythm of the Powers.

"Comrades!" she bellowed. All of a sudden, the mic to the bullhorn, on its snaking black coil, was shoved into her face. Tariq from LWR held both the mic and the bullhorn attached to it. Raquel kept hold of Brenda and Selene's arms. They walked together, forward, toward the Nazis on the street, Tariq walking just ahead, holding the bullhorn itself up high, so the words she spoke into the mic would carry.

Raquel felt the cops and "patriots" behind the coven, along with every person they had organized with, and all of their friends. One body. No separation. They could do this. They could face the white supremacists ahead and behind.

"Comrades!" she said again, this time with amplification. "We are a city of love! We are a city of anger! We are a city that says 'No More!'"

"No more!" the crowd replied.

"We banish these Nazis from our midst and say, 'You are not welcome here!'"

"You are not welcome here!"

The drumming increased its tempo, playing a deep, sexy combination of Ṣàngó and Yemọja's rhythms. Raquel, linked with the coven, danced harder. The coven danced, a sinuous snake of movement and energy. Around them, the people linked arms. The movement rippled through the gathered crowd, until throughout the whole park, everyone had linked with someone else, and everyone was dancing. People in wheelchairs danced. People with their faces covered by black masks danced. People in red and white and black and purple danced.

Yemǫja and Ṣàngó danced through Raquel, and out into the people.

They danced at the white supremacists, the Nazis, the erstwhile patriots filled with hate. They danced at the cops, with their faceplates and shields.

The Powers danced through the people. The people danced for love. For anger. For life.

"You who would say that your whiteness makes you superior!" Raquel danced and shouted into the bullhorn mic. Tariq, eyes bright behind black-rimmed glasses, smiled and danced, backing up now as she moved forward.

"You who would say we don't deserve a safe place to raise our children, and to be happy and free! You are no longer welcome here. This is the people's place! And as long as you choose to stand separate from us, to look down upon us, to beat and crush us...you are not welcome here!"

A mighty roar rose up around her, but the drums held their contrapuntal rhythms, steadily building. Building something bright and dark and true.

"We make the war of love against you!"

Where had those words come from? *Just go with it, Raquel.*

She swayed and stomped with the rhythm, slowly turning the coven in a wheel. The crowd spiraled around them, moving like the sun moved across the surface of the earth.

"The war of love is a long game! But do not mistake it for a weak game!"

The Sons of Ṣàngó surrounded Arrow and Crescent Coven, all of them dancing. They danced their fighting postures. They danced the dance of war.

The coven danced the dance of love.

The whole crowd danced. Danced toward the river and the cops and the Nazis. Danced toward the street and the hate-filled people waiting there, waving their flags and banners and spitting their hate onto the beautiful dance.

Together, love and war—Yemọja and Ṣàngó—danced. The crowd turned, and turned again.

And then Raquel saw them. Three massive flags, waving back and forth, stiffened by the wind from the river. One flag replaced the American stars with crossed Confederate stripes. The other was a simple white flag with a blue pyramid and just one word: *Europa.*

And the third flag, more chilling still, a Black Sun formed from a series of S runes in a ring. Symbol of the victory of the Nazis, and their esoteric power.

"Push them back!" Raquel screamed into the black mic. "Dance!"

The crowd roared again.

Raquel turned her head to Brenda and Selene. "Okay! We have to coordinate this now. We have to do the banishing, working with the power of the crowd. Are you ready?"

Selene looked grim, but nodded.

"Ready," Brenda said. "Let's get the rest of the coven on board."

Raquel kept dancing, arms linked. She kept the rhythm steady as, down the arc, her coven conferred, getting ready to strike.

"Hold on tight," she said to Tariq. "Shit's about to go down."

"Good shit?" he asked.

"Good shit," she replied, then sent out a prayer that her words were true.

38

CHARLIE

Charlie came to, smelling trampled grass, charred denim, and singed skin. His mouth tasted of blood and ashes. He ran his tongue over his mouth. Sure enough, he had bitten his lip and a couple of his teeth felt loose.

Drum rhythms pounded through the air, and dancing feet vibrated the ground. His head throbbed with it. When in the world had the dancing started?

"Damn," he groaned, struggling to roll over and sit up. But he was on something alternately hard, soft, and lumpy. Tim. Right. And the skin on his back still felt like it was on fire. Moving carefully, he extricated himself from the heathen's prone form, and closed his eyes for a moment.

He sure hoped Tim was going to be okay.

"Hey! I have some water. Let me help you!"

A voice he didn't recognize. Charlie peeled his eyes open. A masked face stared down at him. One of the Snack Bloc? They shook a bottle of water in question. He nodded. The person took the cap off and held it up to Charlie's lips. It tasted good. He took another big mouthful, rinsed, leaned away from Tim, and spat onto the grass.

"Thanks," he said.

Charlie looked around. Hai was sitting on the ground, Sam crouched next to him. They seemed okay, though Sam was going to have a shiner, and Hai looked like he had a bruised jaw.

The masked person offered water to Sam and Hai, who both took it, then squatted back down next to Charlie.

"A street medic is coming," she said.

"I don't..."

"He needs one," Sam interrupted. "Your back is burned, Charlie. Tim needs to be looked at, too."

Tim groaned, then rolled to his side and vomited on the grass, then shoved himself upright.

"Motherfucker," Tim said. "Water?"

The black-clad, masked savior proffered another bottle. She seemed to have an endless supply in the messenger bag slung cross body from one shoulder.

"The runes?" Tim croaked out.

"Not sure. The whole ring fell, I think," Charlie replied. At least, that was what he remembered before blacking out from the pain. "How did they get through in the first place, though?"

The ring had been set to protect the crowd from the white supremacists and cops.

"Sowilo," Tim croaked. "They were wearing SS patches. Sowilo was behind us in the ring. Must've been a weak point."

Damn. The Nazis had twisted the rune of sun and brightness and health and growing plants and everything else that was good on earth. They'd turned it into a symbol of terror and pain.

"Got any aspirin?" Tim asked the masked person.

"Let the medics get here and take a look at your legs. They'll have aspirin. All I have are snacks."

Charlie closed his eyes again, listening to the shouting. The dancing. The whole, crazy, maelstrom of activity.

C'mon, Thor. Help me out.

He ran his hands over the grass, trying to recapture the feeling of his blood, and Tim's, charging up the ring, slamming the power outward. What had Moss and Alejandro told him to do?

Slow your breathing and soften your attention.

So he tried.

"Medics are here!" said Sam.

Two people, red tape crosses on their black jackets and messenger bags, red bandanas over their mouths, crouched down, one near Tim and Charlie, the other by Sam and Hai.

The drumming and dancing continued: behind him, toward the cops and the river; in front of him, toward Naito Parkway. Charlie felt the energy build throughout the park. He could practically taste Raquel in it, taste her coffee and the warmth of her skin. When had that happened? The ability to sense people like this?

He shook his head. Pain. That was a mistake. Damn.

C'mon, Thor!

"Can I look at your back?" the medic said.

Then the buzzing, tingling, *knowing* flooded back into Charlie, rolling through his body like thunder. Thor. The runes were still there.

"Not right now. There's something I need to do." He turned to Tim, who finally had a little color coming back into his cheeks. "You okay to do a little magic, man?"

Tim swallowed, then nodded. "As long as I don't have to stand up."

"Thor says we can call him in, and that'll reactivate the ring."

Tim gave a weak grin, took another sip of water and coughed.

"Sounds good to me," he said, once he'd cleared his windpipe.

"Okay," Charlie said. "Medics, Sam, Hai, Snack Bloc? We're gonna need your help, if you're willing. All you have to do is hold hands or link arms with me and Tim. We're gonna channel Thor."

And Thor was gonna kick some Nazi ass.

39

RAQUEL

"You bitch!" The man practically spat in Raquel's face, shoving Tariq out of the way.

"Fuck you, Nazi fucker!" Tariq shouted, trying to shove the man away from Raquel and the rest of the coven.

"Back off, boy, my beef's not with you."

"I'm not your boy."

It was the man who had punched her outside Owlbear.

The man who had sent his son's friends after Zion, and beaten her beautiful boy to a pulp.

Her eyes went black with rage. The sound of pounding surf blocked up her ears.

"Coven! Stop!" she bellowed. She blinked. Her eyes refocused, staring at his ugly, sneering white face.

Arrow and Crescent stopped moving. Raquel felt them all root into the earth and reach up toward the sky. The witch's strongest power was connection to this world. Linked with the great above and below. Linked with each other. Unstoppable force.

"How. Dare. You!" she spat out. "How *dare* you threaten me! How *dare* you send your children *after my son!*"

Yemọja poured through her. All that pounding ocean roared into her arms. Raquel ripped herself from Selene and Brenda's grasp. Her hands snapped up, palms out, toward the man's face. Raquel *shoved* her energy toward him. He staggered backwards, a wild look in his eyes. She smelled piss. A dark stain spread down his camo pants.

"Get out of my way, human," she said. "Take your Nazi friends and go."

Raquel crooked two fingers, pointing the vee toward his eyes. "You're marked by witches now. Touch anyone else? We *will* track you down. Haunt your dreams. Shrivel your dick. Make you wish you hadn't messed with a Black woman and her child."

"Fuck you," he said, voice flat, eyes terrified. Then he turned and walked away.

Raquel took in a heaving breath and dropped her right arm, clenching and unclenching her hand.

"Damn, woman," Tariq said, respect in his eyes. "You ever need backup for *anything*, you got me."

She gave him a tight smile, shook out her hands, then turned to Selene.

There was still work to be done. Not all the white supremacists were gone.

"Ready to do this?"

"Ready," they said.

She looked to Brenda, wavy brown hair falling from its messy bun, framing her beautiful face.

"Ready," Brenda said.

"Tariq?"

He held the bullhorn mic back up in front of Raquel's lips, so close she could almost kiss it.

She filled her lungs, and pitched her voice to carry over the sound of the drums. Felt Selene and Brenda link their arms in hers. Felt the dancers. The drummers. The magic embedded in every living thing.

Felt the river. Yemọja.

"Ban-ish Na-zis!" she yelled into the mic. "Ban-ish hate!"

Since the crowd had already keyed into that chant, she could easily use it to raise power for the working.

She chanted to the rhythm of the drums and began to move her feet in the pattern of the dance of love and war.

The crowd, bursting with energy, chanted with her.

"Ban-ish Na-zis! Ban-ish hate!"

Selene worked their magic. To maintain connection with the coven, Raquel slid her arm behind Selene's back, keeping in contact with the witch. She felt Moss's hand grasp hers from the other side.

Selene's ghostly hands traced sigils in the air, silver rings flashing in the sun.

"Ban-ish Na-zis! Ban-ish hate!"

The drums and chanting filled everything. The coven drew down the power of the sun and breathed up the power of earth. Raquel wove in the power of the river. Brenda wove in the wind. The whole coven poured their power into the magic Selene wove.

"Ban-ish Na-zis! Ban-ish hate!"

Raquel began to shout into the bullhorn microphone, over the chanting and the drums, strengthening the spell. Invoking the Powers.

"Mama! Be with us! Cleanse our city of this hatred! Pour your healing waters through minds. Clear out the poisons that fill our hearts! Yemọja! Mother Ocean! Great River! Flow through me! Flow through us!"

"Ban-ish Na-zis! Ban-ish hate!"

The Sons of Ṣàngó began a chanting counterpoint to her invocation and the chanting of the crowd.

"Ṣàngó Ṣàngó. Bring the lightning! Ṣàngó Ṣàngó. Bring the lightning!"

The three strands wove themselves together with the drums. Pushing back at the Nazis. Pushing back at the cops. Pushing back at fear. Hatred. Oppression. Dominance.

Raquel danced the magic. Selene's hands cast the symbols in the air.

The Confederate flags. The "Don't Tread on Me" flags. The Europa flags. The Black Sun. Tyr's spear, thrusting upward, red on a yellow background, a twisted form of justice. All of it, twisted. Perverted. Wrong.

Raquel could see them all backing up. Receding.

The people danced, and stomped, and swayed. The drums grew loud in Raquel's ears.

She smelled salt water and smoke. Tasted sweet corn cakes.

And smiled.

40

CHARLIE

It was the strangest thing Charlie had ever seen. The crowd was *dancing*. They danced in a flow around Charlie and Tim, followed by the riot cops, and the damn "patriots." The medics, the stalwart Snack Bloc anarchist, and Sam and Hai, stood around Tim and Charlie, forming a wedge. The cops and white supremacists parted like a wave around them, which was something of a miracle.

They had all been braced for another conflict. There had to have been some sort of intervention. Cops in riot gear were not known for being kind to people wearing bandanas over their faces, especially when they were trying to get a crowd to move.

Thor? Charlie asked inside his mind.

:—:

Charlie felt a ping, an almost thought, more of a feeling. It was enough. Enough to convince him the God had something to do with the aura of protection around the tiny group.

Charlie and Tim sat side-by-side on the grass. The medics had insisted on draping cold wet cloths over Tim's legs where his jeans had burned away—stripping off their own T-shirts to the get the job done. They'd turned Charlie's shirt so the burned part was in front, and soaked the new back to get some coolness on his skin.

Not happy about the refusal of further treatment, the medics had nonetheless agreed to stick around and help for a few minutes.

"It can't be too long, though," said one of the medics, a burly guy, bandana still on, exposed torso pasty white, dappled with sun and shade from the cherry trees. "We need to be mobile, in case anyone else needs us. And we'll only help you if you agree to get to urgent care after this."

Charlie only half listened to the medic, aware that Thor was feeding him information the whole time the earnest anarchist was speaking. Thor had a plan. It came to Charlie in flashes of images and sound. He could see what was needed, but wasn't one-hundred-percent certain they could pull it off.

"Deal," Charlie finally said to the medic, just to shut him up. He appreciated the guy's concern, but there were more immediately important things to deal with right now than their burns. "Okay. We need to throw the ring up around the crowd. And Tim? You have to help me focus it so the runes draw on the power they had before the Nazi fuckheads took them over. You're the one with the long-term relationship."

Tim gave him a look. "And you're the one with a direct line to Thor. I'd say we're at least even, dude."

Charlie shrugged, then snapped back to attention, blocking out the pain.

"Ready?" he asked the rest of the group. They nodded. "All you need to do is keep people away from us, and imagine lending us some of your power. Your life energy. Draw on the river and the park if you need to. Tim and I are pretty weak, but luckily the rune ring didn't go away completely. Thor says we just have to draw it back up from the earth."

At least, he hoped so. He had no idea what the hell he was doing. Flying on instinct would hopefully be good enough.

Charlie let that buzzing, humming sense of Thor's presence surround him. The drums and shouting and foot stomping and bullhorns all receded. There was just grass. And the whisper of the runes.

He felt Tim beside him, and clasped the man's hand. He felt Hai and Sam and the others, standing strong and tall. Warriors. Lovers. Friends. He let the feeling of the dancing and drums weave back into the mix. Then he reached. Pulled.

And the runes were there. Slipping through his hands. Pulsing in his mind. But he couldn't raise them.

:———: That *push* at the back of his skull again. Almost words, but not quite. Then an image.

"We need to call the lightning."

"Got it," Tim replied.

Over the sound of drums, shouting, and chanting, Tim called out to the sky.

"Mighty Thor! God of thunder and lighting! We call on you now! Protect the people! Help us raise the runes!" Then Tim turned to Charlie. "Pull!"

They began to pull down the power of the sky. Thor's power. Thor's sky power could raise the runes embedded in the earth. Sweat popped up on Charlie's forehead. He pulled with all his might. He pulled with his imagination. With his energy. With his heart and will and mind.

The drumbeats changed, becoming more staccato. Charlie's ears picked out snatches of intertwined words, chanted in cadence. One of the voices sounded like Raquel's.

He heard the word "lightning," and followed the rhythm, beginning to rock back and forth on his crossed legs. Every movement caused his back to scream with pain. He didn't care. They had to do this.

They needed more energy.

"Stomp!" he shouted to Sam.

She immediately caught the percussive rhythm with her boots. Hai and the medics followed suit.

Dark clouds scudded in, blotting out the sun.

"What the...?" he heard one of the medics ask.

No time to answer questions. Charlie refocused his intention.

Together, he and Tim raised their linked hands. Charlie could feel electricity, crackling in the air. A wind blew from the river, hitting his back and whipping his blond hair around his face.

Thor. Please. We need you.

In front of their small, ragged group, Charlie felt as the earth rose what felt like a fraction of an inch, and lightning split the sky. Thunder rolled.

The earth leapt again, and with a crack, lightning and earth struck one another. Then came rain. Then thunder.

Tim laughed, wild-eyed.

"Let's do this!" he screamed into the wind. "Hail Thor!"

Together, they grasped the rune ring in their hands, and, using the power leant to them by Thor, raised it toward the billowing dark sky.

41

RAQUEL

Rain poured over the crowd. Raquel raised her face to the water that had come out of nowhere. This was not a typical Portland late-spring rain. This was...

The Sons of Ṣàngó. They had called the lightning. And Raquel had this vague sense that Charlie was involved somehow, too.

Of course. Thor.

She shook her head, dreadlocks already heavy with the deluge. Wasn't that something? If it turned out a Yoruban Power and a Norse God had teamed up to defeat a bunch of pasty white Nazis, it would be a first.

She supposed even Gods could form alliances. If people could, why not the Powers?

The roar of the storm met the roaring of the crowd. With a crack and a sizzle, Raquel felt it. The rune ring was back. Full power.

"Right on!" Moss whooped. The coven felt it, too.

Raquel, Selene, and Brenda all worked to coordinate with the rest of Arrow and Crescent, the Sons of Ṣàngó, and the vibrant ring of runes that seemed to have tripled in power.

"Push!" Selene yelled.

Raquel felt Yemọja pulsing in her blood, every heartbeat answering the drums. She felt the rain on her face. The power of the people surrounding her. Charlie and his runes. The Gods, Goddesses, and Powers.

:Daughter, it is your time. Claim this moment. Claim your power.:

After a year of uncertainty. A year of dissatisfaction. A year that included fear, anguish, and pain.... Yes. Raquel felt ready.

What had Yemọja said to her, that day she was rolling on the floor, half out of her mind? *Your anger can trap or cleanse you. Your rage can bind you, or set you free. Choose what you desire. Harness the depths of your ocean. The depth of love. Love is the root of your power.*

Rain on her face, feet pounding on the grass, wet and sticky pink cherry blossoms falling around her, cops, Nazis, witches and anarchists, Buddhists and Christian clergy... Raquel breathed it all in. She reached for the root of her desire. Found it. Brought it forth. Brought forth her power.

Her full power.

She would do this. She *was* doing this. For herself. For Zion. For the people of Portland. And damn it, she wasn't going to give up. Not ever again.

"I choose love!" she shouted into the rain-filled sky.

Tariq shoved the bullhorn mic in front of her mouth. "Say it again!" he yelled.

"I. Choose. Love!" she shouted.

"We. Choose. Love!" the crowd replied, voices booming from the river to the street, and filling up every space between. "We. Choose. Love!"

"Push!" Selene screamed.

Raquel gathered the power of river and ocean, the power of òrìṣà and woman. The power of love. She linked the energy of crowd and the coven and, throwing them at the shining ring of runes, *pushed*, with all her might.

She felt the coven pushing alongside her. With a flash, Selene's spell of banishing locked itself into place. The rune ring flared.

The Nazi flags caught fire, sizzling and burning in the rain. How was that even possible?

The Nazis, white supremacists, and "patriots" screamed as the patches on their clothing caught fire.

Some of the cops screamed, too, behind their masks.

:*Anything is possible*.: Yemọja said. Anything. Even rain and lightning on a sunny day. Even fires burning in the rain.

The white supremacists turned and ran, dropping flag-poles and signs.

And as if she hadn't seen enough, it looked as if the runes chased after them, ready to hunt them down.

Lightning cracked. Rain poured down. Thunder rolled.

The drummers smacked their palms on skin. Once. Twice. Three times.

The rhythm stopped.

The rain stopped.

The crowd stopped. Panting. Wet hair sticking to cheeks or standing out in tufts.

The police stood down. One barked order spread down the line. They backed up one step. Then two. Then walked in formation, away from the park.

Some people laughed, hugging one another. Others cried. Still others looked around, bewildered.

Tariq put the bullhorn mic up to his own mouth, and began a new chant.

"Na na nah na. Na na nah na. Hey Nazis! Goodbye!"

Someone busted out a tuba and joined in.

The crowd began to chant and dance along with Tariq. He smiled at Raquel. She grinned back.

"Na na nah na. Na na nah na. Hey Nazis! Goodbye!"

Raquel, Selene, and Brenda laughed, and the coven danced in a ring on the grass, joined by the Sons of Ṣàngó, the black-clad anarchists, and preachers in clerical collars.

The only thing that would have made it all more perfect?

If Zion could have been there.

But thank the Gods and Goddesses everyone was safe.

42

CHARLIE

The rain left as suddenly as it had appeared.

Charlie released his final hold on the rune ring. He and Tim collapsed against each other's shoulders.

"Charlie! Are you okay?" That was Hai.

Charlie couldn't speak. Only nodded.

He had felt it all. Felt Raquel and the coven. Felt the Gods. The lightning. He had felt the rune ring interact with every symbol on the Nazi's clothing and flags. Every twisted form of sowilo, the sun rune, othala, the rune for family and inheritance that Nazis only used to exclude. And finally, tiwaz. The rune for justice. Well, the Nazis were finally getting theirs.

Tim had somehow worked through Charlie's connection to Thor and, together, powered the symbols to twist back on the Nazis every time they tried to use them for ill.

Amazingly, it had worked. He wondered if it would last.

Charlie felt proud and electrified as well as exhausted and sore. His lower back throbbed, growing worse every second, as the adrenaline began to wear off.

"I think we need that urgent care now," he said to Tim.

The crowd was cheering.

And there she was. The most beautiful woman he'd ever seen. Raquel, running toward him on the grass, dark hair heavy with rain, worry, love, and joy warring on her face.

She practically fell on top of him, clasping her arms tight.

He screamed.

"Oh my Goddess, Charlie!" She scrambled back from him. "What's wrong?"

He winced. "Tim and I got burned."

"We have to get you to the hospital!" she said.

"We've been trying to tell him that," one of the medics replied.

Charlie gave a weak wave. "Yeah. I know. Tim, too."

Then he looked into those gorgeous brown eyes. "But first? Can you please kiss me?"

And she did.

43

RAQUEL

Zion had healed, and Charlie's burns were getting better. Tim's too, slowly.

To say that Raquel felt relieved was an understatement.

Raquel smiled, watching her son slam cupboard doors as he put plates and cups on trays. The door to the backyard was open on a gorgeous day. A Sunday afternoon in Portland in spring. What could be better? She had even changed into a skirt, this one a bright orange with white flowers embroidered around the hem. It had pockets, and felt good as it swirled around her bare legs. Her dreads were down, and the new Yemọja necklace she'd strung together over the last week rested just beneath her collarbone.

Alternating beads of blue and clear crystal, the necklace felt right there. *She* felt right, wearing it. It felt like a promise to Yemọja that Raquel wasn't going anywhere. That she would honor that Power for the rest of her days.

"Is the whole coven coming over?" Zion asked.

"Yep," she replied. "Cassiel and I got folks to cover the café, and Brenda closes early on Sundays, so she and Tempest will both be by around four-thirty. Some of the

Wyrd Sisters are coming, too, and the Sons of Ṣàngó should be by later, for dessert. They had a competition or something today."

Life seemed as if it was getting better, too. Not only were Zion's ribs healed, he was pretty excited about his new-found relationship with Ṣàngó, and with studying martial arts, though Raquel had extracted a promise from Shawn that they'd be careful with him until she was sure Zion's ribs were completely okay.

Along with the coven, Zion was pretty excited that Charlie was coming over for the barbecue. He'd been dropping little comments for the past couple of days.

Raquel was excited, too. She was even allowing herself to get her hopes up. The sex was good, he was kind, and he treated her son with respect. Her, too. They hadn't reached the sleepover stage—always tricky to navigate with a kid involved—but she felt confident they'd figure that out, soon.

It was amazing what two people could do together even when they had to avoid putting pressure on a bandaged back.

The doorbell rang.

"I'll get it!"

Zion raced through the swinging door into the living room. She heard his voice, joined by Lucy, Moss, and Alejandro's. The kitchen door swung open, and her coven mates entered, arms laden with bags of chips, a large bowl of salad, and three bottles of wine.

She smiled. "Bring it all on through to the backyard. There's a long table set up."

For the next half hour, more people kept arriving. She got the barbecue started.

And then Charlie swung open the little gate to the side of the house. Her heart about stopped in her chest before it resumed beating again. She dropped the tongs she'd been using to turn the chicken sausages and grilled peppers, and, wiping her hands on a towel tucked in her back pocket, she walked toward him. He had a watermelon in one arm and a six-pack of ale in the other hand.

"I'd hug you, but..." he said.

"How about a kiss instead?" she asked, smiling, before leaning toward him. He bent his head down, and kissed her long and slow.

She broke the kiss first, aware that she had a yard full of friends and her son. But she didn't want to.

"Food's over here," she said. "Come on in."

She felt the flow of water moving through her hips as she walked, and was aware of Charlie's gaze on her.

"Charlie!" Alejandro said. He was neatly dressed as always, despite just being in jeans and a pink shirt with the sleeves rolled up, baring his light brown arms. Raquel swore Alejandro even starched his T-shirts.

He grabbed the watermelon from Charlie, then went into the kitchen for a knife.

Charlie *snicked* open a beer.

"Where's Zion?" he asked.

Raquel looked around the yard. Where *was* Zion? "In the kitchen, maybe? He's around."

As she spoke, her son came out of the house, grinning wildly, hands behind his back, as if he was hiding something. She smiled back at him, knowing just what it was. Her resourceful son had asked Brenda for a special order. Brenda's girlfriend, Caroline—a gemstone and jewelry dealer—was the one who finally tracked it down. He even used his saved-up allowance money for it, though she had pitched in to make up the difference.

"Hey, Zion! It's good to see you!" Charlie set his beer on

the table and walked toward her son, hand outstretched to shake. Zion held out his fisted hands, palms down, instead.

"Pick," her son said.

Charlie paused and made a big show of stroking his chin, considering. The rest of the coven filtered over, watching. Brenda and Caroline stood to the side, arms around each other, smiles on their faces.

Charlie reached out his right hand, allowing it to hover over first one, then the other of Zion's closed fists.

He's been learning from the witches, Raquel thought. That was an old trick, figuring out where energy was concentrated by sensing it through an open palm.

"That one," Charlie said, tapping Zion's left hand. Zion turned his hand face up and opened it.

"Oh man," Charlie said. "That's beautiful."

"Pick it up," Zion said.

It was a forged steel Thor's hammer. Not the traditional one that heathens usually wore. This one looked more like the hammer from the *Avengers* comic books. A small sledge with squared-off edges. Somehow, Zion had seen it online, and Caroline, with her connections in the jewelry world, had been able to track it down.

"I love it, man," Charlie said. Then he opened out his arms. Zion stepped into them. Charlie and her son gripped each other in a hug and Raquel's eyes filled with tears.

She thought back to that day at the ocean, which seemed like a year ago, but was really less than one month. Raquel's fingers closed around the blue beach glass in her skirt pocket. She remembered her prayer to the ocean that day.

Her wish had come true. Not only did she have her power back, the love she already had in her life had only increased. And her heart had expanded to include one more.

Thank you, mother.

Raquel wrapped her arms around Charlie and Zion. They opened up, making a huddle of three.

It felt a lot like family. And like the possibility of a new kind of home.

REVIEWS

Reviews can make or break a book's success.
If you enjoyed this book, please consider telling a friend, or
leaving a short review at your favorite booksellers or on
GoodReads.
Many thanks!

Look for the next book in the series: By Moon

Visit thorncoyle.com for a free short story collection and to sign up for a monthly newsletter.

T. THORN COYLE
AUTHOR OF THE PANTHER CHRONICLES
BY
MOON
THE WITCHES OF PORTLAND
BOOK FIVE

BY MOON

The scent of oil paint, turpentine, and linseed made Selene feel at home, chasing away any sense of unease they'd carried into the studio. The lights from the Morrison Bridge winked outside the chipped frames of the warehouse windows, lighting up the span and casting bright globes that sparkled on the waters of the Willamette.

The large studio space was quiet, the only sounds being the soft whoosh of cars heading toward the bridge, some laughter from the bar on the corner, and the tinny sound of music played too loud in someone's earbuds.

Only two other people were in the whole shared arts complex. People had better things to do at ten o'clock on a Friday night in June. It had been a hot day at the tail of a scorching week, which meant the patio bars and outdoor cafés would be doing brisk business. Considering the sun didn't set until 9 pm this time of year, and light faded later still, only a fool would be inside by choice.

Well, Selene was one of those fools. Happy to have found a studio they could afford, and driven inside by the will to paint. And the need to escape that sinking feeling in the pit of their gut they'd been carrying around for the past few weeks.

Something was wrong and Selene hadn't been able to pinpoint what. Oh, there was the backwash from the coven fighting off white supremacists the month before. The fallout from that was going to take time to settle, both in the coven and in the city itself. They'd won that battle, but were under no illusions that they'd won the war.

And then Selene had to defend their thesis in order to graduate, which had been frankly harrowing. Because of a disagreement with their advisor, Selene almost didn't make it through.

After that, a person would think that Selene would take a break, but the opposite was true. Selene needed to prove to themself and their muse that art was paramount, grades and degrees or no.

Besides, art was often the only thing keeping Selene alive.

There had been way too much despair lately. Trans friends resorting to suicide to stop the hurting inflicted on them by a world that could not comprehend their beauty. Black boys murdered. Indigenous women missing. Hate crimes of all types on the rise. And Selene?

Selene was just a non-binary Goth femme, longing for love and not knowing where to find it. Or if they could even take the risk.

Love required too much exposure. Body and soul. That was the hardest thing about completing their thesis. Their advisor kept pushing Selene to dig deeper. To show more of themself.

That was how great art was made, Ms. Monroe said. "You bare your soul to the canvas and paint it with your spit and blood."

Those were stirring words that sounded great in theory. But then Selene had to put them into practice and it really had about killed them. They'd skipped the graduation ceremony, and had only crawled out from the aerie of their attic home a week ago, anxious to get brush in hand again.

Luckily, Art Commons Collective had studio space available for non-members on a drop-in basis. Selene was trying it out, figuring they could always join in a month or two if they liked it. So far, they did.

The space was good, the people seemed nice, and left Selene alone, which was a good thing. Selene needed to ease into new social situations slowly.

Selene realized they'd been staring at the canvas, unseeing, for who knew how long. They sighed, then refocused on the still life taking shape. It was such a relief to paint something that, while it revealed something of the artist, didn't feel as if it were flaying them alive in the process.

So here Selene was, just post-graduation, with a fresh degree in graphic design, minor in fine art. Graphic design was interesting and paid the bills, and painting filled their soul.

The best paintings always drew them inside, working Selene like a perfectly executed magic spell, or a favorite song, thrumming through their body on a crowded dance floor.

But that was neither here nor there. Selene had this painting to complete. It was a challenging enough piece, an occult still life that attempted to convey the deeper mystery behind the objects gathered on the scarred, walnut table. The deer skull. A black handled knife. A spray of foxglove. And a chalice, painted as if it reflected a rising moon.

Limning a bright line along the edge of the deer's skull, Selene tried to tune into the painting again. The moon was almost full. Selene could feel it. They had always been attuned to the moon. Their childhood fascination with the glowing orb is what led Selene to witchcraft, and, of course, to their name.

Selene, Goddess of the moon. Daughter of Titans, sister of the sun.

Selene had been raised by ordinary, flawed humans, and was an only child, but they felt as if they *could* be sibling to the sun. Maybe. Mostly though, even though the full moon was gorgeous, Selene tucked themself away like the moon behind the perpetually cloudy Portland skies.

Besides, darkness was good for a lot of the magic it turned out Selene was best at. Bindings. Uncrossings. Banishings. Oh, they could work the mechanics of prosperity or love spells, and of course collaborated with their coven on spells for justice, but...they were just more comfortable with working magic on the dark side of the moon.

Cassiel would give Selene shit if she knew her coven mate wasn't comfortable doing magic for themself. Not after Selene had given Cassie a hard time for not asking the Gods for help with her own little situation last winter.

They rubbed a long hand across their forehead, careful not to smudge any paint on their skin. Selene spent too much time on their makeup to mar it with the thick paint that slicked the horsehair brush.

Arrow and Crescent coven a good fit for a witch dedicated to the moon. Coven members all had different deity affiliations, but the coven itself was dedicated to Diana, another Goddess with ties to the moon.

It was funny, gazing at the moon always grounded Selene more firmly on earth. It reminded them that they were on a rock in the middle of space, and that the rock was home. Just like Portland was, and likely always would be, home.

They stepped back from the painting a moment, trying to see the whole. The bright edge of the skull reflected the moon in the water. The blade edge needed drawing out to form a magic triangle created by the lines of light. A triangle of edges.

Just like Selene.

Sometimes it really felt as if they were nothing but edge. No center. No core. No soft beating heart. No warm lips. No laughter.

It was as if Selene had been built to be a weapon. A sharp sword to be wielded against those who intended harm.

It wasn't a good feeling. Never had been.

Selene was a sharp sickle, not the lush fullness of the moon that practically set her long, dark hair afloat around her head.

"Fuck. May as well pack it in for the night," they murmured. Once this mood hit, there was nothing to do but drink, or dance, have sex, or sleep. No way were they ready for bed, and sex? Yeah, unless it was with Selene's own hand, that wasn't happening. Social anxiety made that a minefield they just weren't up to navigating right now.

"Drink and dance it is, then," Selene said. Setting the brush in the soaking jar, they began to scrape the paint off their palate.

"I just hope you know what you're up to, moon."

Selene felt the small hairs on their arms stand up, as if something had just walked over their grave. They whipped their head around, looking for danger. Nothing. Selene's dark eyes rested on the still life. The water in the chalice on the table moved, rippling for a moment, as though a form attempted to take shape.

A trick of the eye? Or a message to pay attention? All Selene knew was, the studio didn't feel so homey anymore.

"Okay, Goddess. I'm listening. Just let me know what to do."

But please, don't make me be a knife right now. And don't expose me too much. I really need a break.

ACKNOWLEDGMENTS

I give thanks to the cafés of my new hometown, Portland, Oregon. All you baristas are fine human beings.

Thanks also to Leslie Claire Walker, my intrepid first reader, to Dayle Dermatis, editor extraordinaire, to Lou Harper for my covers, and to my writing buddies for getting me out of the house.

Speaking of house...thanks as always to Robert and Jonathan.

Big, grateful shout out to the members of the Sorcery Collective for spreading the word!

And last...

Thanks to all the activists and witches working your magic in the world. This series is for you.

ABOUT THE AUTHOR

T. Thorn Coyle has been arrested at least four times. Buy her a cup of tea or a good whisky and she'll tell you about it.

Author of the *The Witches of Portland*, the alt-history urban fantasy series *The Panther Chronicles*, the novel *Like Water*, and two story collections, her multiple non-fiction books include *Sigil Magic for Writers, Artists & Other Creatives*, and *Evolutionary Witchcraft*.

Thorn's work appears in many anthologies, magazines, and collections. She has taught magical practice in nine countries, on four continents, and in twenty-five states.

An interloper to the Pacific Northwest U.S., Thorn stalks city streets, writes in cafes, loves live music, and talks to crows, squirrels, and trees.

Connect with Thorn:
www.thorncoyle.com

ALSO BY T. THORN COYLE

Fiction Series

The Panther Chronicles

To Raise a Clenched Fist to the Sky

To Wrest Our Bodies From the Fire

To Drown This Fury in the Sea

To Stand With Power on This Ground

The Witches of Portland, a 9 Book Series

By Earth

By Flame

By Wind

By Sea

By Moon...

Single Novels and Story Collections

Like Water

Alighting on His Shoulders

Break Apart the Stone

Anthologies

Fantasy in the City

Haunted

Witches Brew

The Faerie Summer

Stars in the Darkness

Fiction River: Justice

Fiction River: Feel the Fear

Non-Fiction

Evolutionary Witchcraft

Kissing the Limitless

Make Magic of Your Life

Sigil Magic for Writers, Artists & Other Creatives

Crafting a Daily Practice